**"The things she ca
Dan scratched his head. "I've never seen anything like it."**

"She treats them?" Josh asked.

The farmer nodded and lowered his voice. "Looked at an animal or two of mine. Darned if they didn't turn right around and get better, and she barely touched them."

Josh mulled this news over. What was she thinking, that she was some kind of mystical healer? It was so typical of alternative-medicine types to try to meddle where they had no business. Clearly, Gen was no different.

"Well, thanks again, Doc," Dan said, taking Josh's hand in his calloused grip. "Say, she's single." He grinned. "You two could make a pretty good team, if you don't mind my saying so."

Josh said goodbye and slid behind the wheel of the Suburban, ignoring the man's last remark. He was already planning to find out exactly what it was that Genevie Halvorson was doing in Halden.

Dear Reader,

I've always been interested in the conflict between
traditional and alternative medical practices. In
The Baby Season, I drew on my background as a veterinary
technician to illustrate that conflict between vet Josh
McBride and midwife Gen Halvorson. Josh's personal
experience with alternative medicine has caused him to
view the field, and those who practice it, with skepticism
and distrust. For Gen Halvorson, though, alternative
medicine is a way of life and a philosophy she blends
seamlessly with her career as a midwife and her avocation
in wildlife rehabilitation. Through their shared love of
animals, they overcome their differences and their own
painful pasts to find love and create a brand-new family
for Josh's son, Tyler.

The small, close-knit communities of central and eastern
North Dakota, where my husband grew up, inspired the
fictional town of Halden and the surrounding countryside
where *The Baby Season* takes place. Gen's animals, especially
her cats, Scotty and Simba, and Josh's patients at Halden
Veterinary Hospital are based on my own pets and my
experiences working in a veterinary practice. I hope you
have as much fun reading *The Baby Season* as I did writing it.

Sincerely,

Lisa McAllister

The Baby Season

LISA McALLISTER

HARLEQUIN®

TORONTO • NEW YORK • LONDON
AMSTERDAM • PARIS • SYDNEY • HAMBURG
STOCKHOLM • ATHENS • TOKYO • MILAN • MADRID
PRAGUE • WARSAW • BUDAPEST • AUCKLAND

ISBN 0-373-75064-1

THE BABY SEASON

This edition published by arrangement with Harlequin Books S.A.

® and TM are trademarks of the publisher. Trademarks indicated with
® are registered in the United States Patent and Trademark Office, the
Canadian Trade Marks Office and in other countries.

www.eHarlequin.com

Printed in U.S.A.

To my marvelous, talented and patient
critique partners: Carol, Darcy, DeeAnna and Melinda—
friends yesterday, today and tomorrow.

Books by Lisa McAllister

HARLEQUIN AMERICAN ROMANCE
1060—THE BABY SEASON

HARLEQUIN SUPERROMANCE
810—BUFFALO GAL

Chapter One

"Okay, moms, shallow panting breaths. Like this. Huh, huh, huh." Gen Halvorson demonstrated for the five couples settled on mats on the floor of the veterinary hospital waiting room. "Coaches, massage mom's shoulders and neck. Watch that tension. Keep those muscles loose."

She moved among her students in the small space, checking their technique and offering suggestions. To a man, the coaches, all first-time fathers-to-be, applied themselves seriously, expressions rapt, foreheads creased in concentration. Their partners, five moms-to-be in various stages of pregnancy, seemed at ease by comparison.

She'd noticed the phenomenon before in her childbirth classes. The women, although tentative at first, got into the routine almost instinctively. For their husbands, though, the idea of practicing for labor was foreign and more than a little scary. Fortunately, none of the group seemed disturbed at the necessity of holding classes in an animal hospital.

Gen had had plenty of opportunity recently to observe the varied emotions of expectant parents. Halden, North Dakota, and vicinity were in the middle of a major baby boom, compliments of the particularly harsh winter not long past. Tonight's class would be her third this week.

Suddenly tired, she glanced at the clock above the reception desk. Almost seven. A few minutes longer and she'd be done.

"Okay," she said. "Relax and take some deep breaths. In through the nose, out through the mouth."

The door opened and a tall, athletic-looking man stepped inside. He stopped abruptly, a puzzled expression on his handsome face, and leaned back outside to study the sign in front of the building. Then he returned, staring at the couples gathered on the floor. "Excuse me, is this the Halden Veterinary Hospital?"

Before Gen could reply, one of the coaches rose quickly and helped his wife to her feet. "You're in the right place. We were just finishing up. I'm Dr. Matt Connolly, one of the vets here in Halden." He gestured to the attractive, and significantly pregnant, brunette beside him. "My wife, Sue, the other vet, is the reason you're here, unless I miss my guess. Are you Dr. McBride?"

The man nodded and took Matt Connolly's proffered hand, but his eyes lingered on Gen a moment before he turned to the other man. "Josh McBride. Call me Josh. I thought I'd walked into the wrong building. Glad to meet you, Dr. Connolly and—" he paused and smiled at Sue "—Dr. Connolly."

"It's Matt and Sue, please, and no, this is the place. We lost our community-center roof to a tornado last fall and haven't had a chance to complete repairs. Gen's classes have been meeting here in the waiting room after hours." Matt caught Gen's hand to pull her forward. "Genevie Halvorson, meet Josh. Gen's our childbirth instructor and Sue's midwife."

Sue spoke up before Gen could respond. "For heaven's

sake, Matt, don't throw her at him. He just walked in the door." She turned to Gen. "Josh will be our relief vet while I'm on maternity leave."

"Pleased to meet you," Gen said, tipping her head up to meet the cornflower-blue eyes of Josh McBride. Okay, she thought, maybe she could overlook Matt's eagerness to introduce her, just this once.

"My pleasure," Josh said, his voice slightly husky. He shook her hand. His grip was warm, but that didn't prevent a little shiver from running through her at the contact. "Genevie. That's an unusual name."

Gen nodded. "It's a family name, but call me Gen." She felt lost in those deep blue eyes.

"Hey, didn't you say you were bringing your son with you?" Matt asked.

Gen tore her gaze away and reclaimed her hand, irritated yet grateful for the interruption.

"Tyler's asleep in the car," Josh said. "I promised him I'd wake him when we got here, but I wanted to check in first. I'll go get him." He slipped out the door.

Sue Connolly glanced at Gen and raised an eyebrow. "Wow. Kind of a babe, huh?"

"He's not bad," Gen admitted, forcing herself to sound noncommittal. Josh McBride was undoubtedly good-looking, tall and sandy haired. And those eyes. "But I'm not in the market." She stared emphatically at Matt. "So don't even try."

Matt shrugged, his expression all wounded innocence. "Just trying to be helpful."

Gen snorted. "Yeah, well, that kind of help I don't need."

A CHILDBIRTH CLASS in the veterinary clinic waiting room? Josh wondered. An unusual venue, but at least emergency medical equipment would be handy in case of a problem.

He found his thoughts drifting to the petite, red-haired instructor of the class, Gen Halvorson.

He'd always thought likening women to cars was juvenile, but for this one, the comparison worked. She was sleek and compact but lushly curved in all the right places, like a classic Corvette. Her eyes were deep emerald-green under sooty lashes, which somehow seemed appropriate despite the brilliant copper of the long hair she wore pulled back in a ponytail.

An image sprang forcibly to mind of those silken strands flowing through his fingers. He shook off the thought. He was here to do a job, not get involved with the locals, however appealing. A few weeks and he'd be on the road again, probably on the way to a new assignment, so building relationships outside of business was a pointless exercise.

He opened the back door of the old Volvo wagon and shook his sleeping son gently. "Wake up, buddy."

Eight-year-old Tyler sat up, squinting in the glare of the dome light, his hair tousled where it had pressed against the seat. "Are we there?"

"Yep, we're there." Such as it was, Josh thought. Tyler hadn't missed much by sleeping through the sights of Halden, North Dakota: a few low buildings, a bank, several bars, an onion-shaped water tower. Josh had gotten directions to the veterinary clinic that would be his temporary workplace, but he hadn't needed them. It would be hard to get lost in Halden.

Tyler stretched, unfastened his lap belt and clambered out of the car. He looked up and down the main street—

the only street—of Halden and frowned. "Wow, Dad, this is a little town. Do you think they even have cable?"

Josh shrugged. "Don't know. If not, I'm sure we'll find something to keep you busy."

Tyler gave him "the look." "Good thing I brought my Game Boy."

He heaved a resigned sigh and started to drag a duffel bag from the back-seat floor, but Josh stopped him with a hand on his shoulder. "Leave that for now. We need to find out where we're staying."

Tyler shrugged and dropped the bag, then swung the car door closed, slamming it a little harder than necessary.

Josh ignored his son's crankiness as he led the way into the clinic. Tyler was always a bit irritable for the first few days at a new location, even when he hadn't just been awakened from a sound sleep. He soon adapted to the change, however. Josh was grateful that his son took after him in that respect.

As an army brat, Josh has moved frequently as his father received new assignments. Although it had been difficult to leave school and friends each time, he'd made the transitions smoothly and eventually became used to being uprooted on a regular basis. By the time he reached his teens, he'd learned to accept the nomadic routine of his life, avoiding attachments that would make the inevitable separation painful. No doubt Tyler would learn to do the same.

Now that the reception and waiting areas had cleared of pregnant couples, other than the Connollys, Josh noted that the rooms were clean, bright and modern, despite the rustic ambiance of the town itself. He couldn't be certain until he saw the surgery and treatment rooms, but Halden Veterinary Hospital appeared to be reasonably up-to-date.

The front desk even held a computer. Some of the country practices where he'd subbed in the past were still virtually in the Stone Age. He breathed in the medicinal aroma of the place, relaxing for the first time in days.

"This must be Tyler," Matt greeted them, holding out his hand to Josh's son. "I'm Matt, and this is my wife, Sue."

Yawning, Tyler shook hands with the Connollys. "Hi."

"He's not quite awake yet," Josh apologized for his son. "We've been on the road ten hours today, but he just dozed off about an hour ago. He was hoping to stay awake to see what the town looked like."

Gen stepped forward. "You must be exhausted. Hi, Tyler, I'm Gen." She offered her hand, as well. "We'll make sure you get a tour tomorrow when it's light. Not that there's a whole lot to see."

Tyler shook her hand. "Hello," he murmured, staring at Gen, then looking at the floor.

Josh grinned. Apparently, shyness around beautiful women was another of his traits his son shared.

Gen glanced at him before he could wipe the smile from his face, and her creamy cheeks turned rosy. He couldn't remember the last time he'd met a woman who blushed. Josh found it alluring.

"Speaking of tours," Matt said, providing a welcome distraction. "You probably want to see the hospital."

Sue took his arm. "Not tonight, honey. They've been driving all day and they're probably starving to death, too. Let's get on home, have dinner and get them settled for the night. You'll have plenty of time tomorrow to get Josh up to speed."

Matt draped his arm around her shoulders and gave her a squeeze. "Sorry. You're right. It is getting late. You need to eat, too," he said, laying a hand protectively on her rounded tummy. He turned back to Josh. "You'll be staying with us out at our ranch. It's not too far from here. Why don't you follow us in your car?"

"I think Matt's aunt Hilma is frying chicken for dinner tonight," Sue added. She looked at Tyler. "Do you like fried chicken?"

The boy nodded eagerly. "It's my favorite." His gaze dropped to her belly. "Are you going to have a baby?"

Sue grinned. "I sure am."

"When?" Tyler asked.

"Feels like any minute." She flinched slightly, then smiled. "The baby's kicking. Want to feel it?"

Ty's eyes widened and he glanced at Josh.

"I don't think that's necessary," Josh said. His son had spent enough time around veterinary clinics to know the facts of life, at least as far as Josh felt was appropriate, but touching a strange woman's tummy was more exposure to those facts than he needed.

The redhead spoke up. "It's perfectly normal for a child to be curious about pregnancy and childbirth, Dr. McBride. My patients' children often attend the births of their brothers and sisters. It can be a bonding experience for the whole family, and after all, you and Tyler are going to be part of the family around here, at least for a while."

Josh couldn't suppress a spark of annoyance. "Thanks, Ms. Halvorson, but Tyler is only eight years old and I really don't think he needs any more exposure to the birth process. And as for being family, well, that's nice of you, but I'm here to do a job. It's only temporary and I have no intention of becoming part of anything other than a working team."

Gen blinked, clearly taken aback at his words, and Josh realized he'd been harsher than he'd intended.

She simply nodded. "I understand. That's your decision, of course." Whether she meant about Tyler or about being part of the Halden family, she didn't say.

Sue spoke up in the ensuing silence. "Well, shall we head home? Hilma won't keep that chicken hot all night."

"Are you going, too, Gen?" Tyler asked.

Gen nodded. "I rode in with Sue and Matt, so my car is still at the ranch."

"Do you want to ride in our car?" Tyler's invitation took her by surprise.

"That's a good idea," Matt said, before she could politely decline. "You can give Josh directions if we get separated."

Gen glanced at Josh, wishing she could beg off and return with the Connollys, but Matt's suggestion made sense. It wasn't a long drive, but some of the turns were easy to miss in the dark.

Josh McBride's blue eyes were unreadable. Finally he gave a shrug. "That'll work, I guess."

Gen caught the exasperated look he shot Tyler. Clearly Josh wasn't any more thrilled with the prospect than she was, but Tyler was fighting back a grin.

Josh led the way to the car, and she was surprised when he went to the passenger side to open the door for her.

"Thank you." She took her seat.

"No problem," Josh murmured. He opened Tyler's door, then walked to the driver's side to get in.

They waited in silence as Matt helped Sue into their Suburban, then Josh followed the big SUV out of the parking lot.

Tyler spoke up from the back seat. "Dr. Connolly said you're a midwife. What's a midwife?"

Josh answered before she had a chance to reply. "It's a person who helps ladies have their babies."

A vague answer, Gen thought, but one she couldn't argue with. Besides, if his earlier attitude was any indication, Josh would prefer to handle this line of questioning himself.

"Like a doctor?" Tyler persisted.

"More like a nurse," Josh said.

"Do you do anything else besides help ladies have babies?" Tyler directed this question pointedly at Gen.

"Well, helping deliver babies keeps me pretty busy," she replied, "but I'm also an herbalist."

"Oh, that explains it," Josh murmured.

Tyler then asked, "What's an herbalist?"

"Explains what?" Gen turned to Josh, puzzled. To Tyler, she answered, "An herbalist is someone who uses plants to make medicines for people and animals." She looked back at Josh, waiting for an answer.

"All that family-bonding business," he replied. "Are you into that New Age junk, like auras and chakra therapy, or just giving people plant decoctions and false hope when there's nothing that can be done?"

Where had that come from? Gen wondered. She bristled at the implication that she was some sort of charlatan. "It's hardly New Age, Dr. McBride. Midwives and herbalists have been around a lot longer than doctors and veterinarians."

"So have witch doctors," he said coolly.

Gen bit her lip, trying hard to keep from rising to the challenge, but finally couldn't resist. "That's not exactly an enlightened attitude," she said. "Many traditional medical practitioners see value in alternative medicine. The Connollys, for example."

Unfortunately, his point of view wasn't unusual, either. She'd encountered such bias before. This was the first time, though, that she'd felt compelled to defend herself. She'd just met the man; what was it about him that made her want to change his mind?

"I've had some experience with so-called alternative medicine," he said. "I'll stick with the real thing."

He looked at her, and for a moment she could see a flicker of pain in his blue eyes. Then it was gone, as he returned his attention to the road and the Connollys' vehicle ahead of them.

Gen stared out the window into the night. She could feel the tension radiating from Josh McBride and imagined that if she turned to face him, she'd see it pulsating around his body like the auras he derided. He had lost someone close to him, she realized. How long ago had it been?

Tyler had subsided back into his seat, having apparently lost interest now that the grown-ups had taken over the conversation.

Josh glanced at his son in the rearview mirror. Watching Ty, and with all the talk of childbirth, Josh recalled the night his son was born, letting the memory of the love and wonder he'd experienced replace his annoyance at Gen Halvorson.

He'd been so scared. Kathy had been scared, too, and in pain, but she had teased him nonetheless. The big, brave vet who delivered breech foals with one hand tied behind his back, but got nervous at the thought of sitting through his own child's birth. Her labor progressed quite rapidly for the birth of a first child, but at the time it had seemed to go on for an eternity.

He'd cringed at each contraction that racked her body,

determined that if she could tolerate what she was suffering, the least he could do was stay with her through it all. He had, and they'd cried together as Tyler made his entrance, kicking and screaming, into the world.

That had been eight years ago. Kathy had been gone for three.

He'd had a good job in a busy Seattle practice when she was diagnosed with leukemia. The progress of the disease was rapid. When traditional medicine failed, they'd grasped desperately at alternative treatments, the practitioners of which eagerly offered hope for a cure. For a price, of course. When those treatments failed, as well, they'd pressed Kathy to try new options. Unwilling to give up hope, fearing to lose her, he'd encouraged her to keep trying until at last, exhausted and resigned, she'd told him "no more." She'd died, peacefully, a few days later.

Afterward, anxious to escape the memories, he'd left the practice to take a job filling in for a vacationing veterinarian in another city. He'd moved himself and Tyler, then five, barely thinking twice before leaving Seattle.

Another assignment had followed that one, then another, and so on until he'd lost track of the clinics where he'd temporarily worked. In the rare breaks between jobs, he and Tyler returned to Seattle, making that their unofficial base of operations since it was near Ty's grandparents.

Josh forced back the torrent of memories. He'd done his grieving and moved on, literally. Now he was here in Halden, getting ready to fill in for yet another veterinarian, then pick up and move again when the job was finished.

He glanced at Gen Halvorson, noting the stiff set of her shoulders as she faced away from him, looking out the window. He'd been kind of rough on her. Again. They had met barely an hour ago and he had already acted like a jerk twice. That had to be a record, even for him.

He followed the Connollys' Suburban as it turned off the road onto an unpaved stretch that looked, and rode, like an old cow track. Oddly, the big SUV sped up on the rough surface. Matt Connolly seemed to be in a hurry, all of a sudden. Josh wondered why but kept the wagon's speed steady. He wasn't likely to lose them on the flat, straight road. No need to shake the old vehicle, or its occupants, apart.

He shot another quick glance at Gen. She probably had a stiff neck to go with those taut shoulders. Wasn't stubbornness a redhead characteristic? Or was that temper? So far she'd maintained her temper pretty well in the face of his provocation. He considered his own attitude and realized Gen Halvorson wasn't the only stubborn one in the car.

Maybe he should apologize, he thought. After all, he'd probably see her around. Halden was a small town, plus she'd be out at the ranch frequently tending to Sue Connolly. It wouldn't hurt to be civil, regardless of the differences in their medical philosophies.

"Gen—"

The trill of a cell phone cut him off. Gen reached into her bag to pull out the phone. She glanced at the screen, then held it to her ear.

"Matt? What's up?" She nodded. "Okay, go ahead and get her home. It's just a couple minutes. We're right behind you."

She turned to Josh, the worry in her green eyes belying her outward calm. "Sue's gone into labor."

Chapter Two

A wave of adrenaline rushed through Josh at her words. No wonder Matt was speeding over the rough road. Josh knew from both his medical training and his own experience that they probably had plenty of time before the actual delivery, but logic didn't diminish his gut reaction. Besides, based on his schedule for the job at Halden, it was a few weeks till Sue Connolly's due date. A premature birth could very well constitute an emergency.

Josh followed the Connollys' vehicle through a white-painted gate topped with a sign proclaiming Lilac Hills Ranch.

At first glance, the ranch looked like those he'd seen during his other temp jobs. On closer inspection, however, he realized that the woolly animals clustered near the fences, dark shapes against the moonlit brightness of the night, were not grazing cattle, but bison.

Tyler made the discovery at the same time. "Dad, look! Buffaloes!"

"I see them. This must be a buffalo ranch." He glanced at Gen for confirmation.

She turned her worried face from the Suburban ahead of them and nodded, seeming grateful for the distraction.

"That's right. Lilac Hills is pretty well known around here. A rare white buffalo calf was born just last season, so they have a lot of visitors to see her."

"Cool! I've seen buffaloes at the zoo, but never a white one," Tyler said. "They're really called bison, you know. Not buffaloes. Buffaloes live in Asia. We learned that in school."

"That's true," Gen replied. "It sounds like you know a lot about them."

"Yeah." Tyler accepted the compliment humbly. "They're pretty neat. Are white bison really white?"

"They're usually more of a creamy color," Gen said, turning to face the boy.

Josh noted that Gen talked to Tyler like an equal instead of in the patronizing manner adults often used with kids. He knew his son would appreciate that.

He didn't mean to tune out their conversation, but his attention turned to the house they were approaching. The kind of farmhouse he'd always dreamed of owning, the rambling white two-story had a wraparound porch and a sweeping view of the plains. If Kathy had lived, they'd have had a house like this someday, a place of their own where they could watch their children grow.

He broke off the thought as Matt pulled to a stop in front.

"Just pull in alongside them," Gen directed.

Josh obeyed and Gen leaped from the car as soon as they came to a halt, rushing to assist Sue.

"Is she having her baby now?" Tyler asked.

"It looks that way." Josh climbed out of the car and Tyler followed. Feeling somewhat at a loss, he stepped up behind Gen, motioning Tyler to wait by the car. "Is there anything I can do?"

Gen held up a hand, her attention on her watch as she timed Sue's current contraction. After a moment she spoke. "I think this is probably false labor, Sue, maybe Braxton Hicks contractions. We need to get you up to bed, though, just to be safe, and I don't want you walking." She turned to Josh and Matt, who'd come around to Sue's side of the SUV and stood looking on anxiously. "Can one of you carry her into the house?"

Sue shook her head. "Don't be silly. It's not going to be that much of a strain for me to walk up the stairs. I'm certainly not going to have someone carry me, especially Matt after his back injury a couple months ago."

"My back's fine," Matt said. "Gen's right. If this is a premature labor, and not a false labor, the less physical exertion till you're stabilized, the better. Carrying you into the house isn't going to kill me."

"What kind of injury was it?" Josh asked.

The other veterinarian shrugged, his expression a little sheepish. "Horse stepped on me during a call last winter. It was no big deal. A couple months on anti-inflammatories and I was good as new."

Sue gave an exasperated sigh. "It stepped on him after knocking him on his face. The injury was a compression fracture of the lumbar spine." She gave her husband a pointed look. "You're not carrying me."

"She's right, Matt," Josh said. "I'm surprised you didn't need a relief vet yourself. I'll carry her."

Gen looked at Josh, the surprise in her green eyes giving way to warmth. "Good. Now that that's settled, let's get her inside. It's cold out here."

Josh stepped forward and slid one arm behind the pregnant woman's back and the other under her knees, then gently lifted her from the vehicle. She was tall but slender, and even at nearly nine months' pregnant, she wasn't heavy.

"Oh, for heaven's sake," Sue commented, but resignedly draped an arm around Josh's neck. "I could have at least stood up on my own."

"No, you couldn't," Matt, Josh and Gen responded in unison.

Matt led the way into the house, followed by Josh and Sue, then Tyler, carrying his duffel bag. Gen hung back, making a call on her cell phone.

An older woman, wiry and weathered with a puff of lavender hair, met them at the door. "What on earth happened?" she asked upon seeing Josh with Sue. "Is she hurt?"

"She's fine, Hilma," Matt assured the woman. "Looks like it could be premature labor, though, and Gen wants her put to bed till we know for sure." He turned to Josh. "Follow me. I'll make introductions when we come back down."

"Stay down here, Ty," Josh said over his shoulder. "I'll be right back."

"Come along to the kitchen, young fella." Hilma turned to Tyler, nearly succeeding in covering her concern with a smile. "I've got some cocoa warming up. I'll bet you're hungry, too."

Assured that Ty was in good hands, Josh carried Sue up the steep steps to a large bedroom where Matt was propping pillows against the headboard of the bed.

"Just set me down anywhere," Sue said. "I can get in bed by myself."

"Nothing doing," Josh replied, smiling. "I have my orders." He deposited her gently on the bed, where Matt helped her get settled.

"Darn straight," Gen spoke behind him. "Sue, you're not

setting foot on the floor till we know what we're dealing with here." She stepped forward and took the other woman's wrist, monitoring her pulse. "Still having contractions?"

Sue nodded. "They don't seem to be getting worse or any more frequent, though. Maybe fifteen minutes apart. Will you be able to stop the labor, if that's what it is?"

"I don't know," Gen replied. "It's a good sign that the contractions aren't increasing in frequency or in strength, though. I called your OB. She'll be here as soon as she can. She'll do an exam and may put you on meds to stop the contractions if you are in labor. In the meantime, I want to check for dilation."

"Guess that's my cue to leave." Josh moved toward the door.

"I'll be down in a minute," Matt said. "Make yourself at home." He turned back to Gen. "If you can't stop the contractions, what's next?"

"Delivery, probably. Fortunately, Sue's not too far from her scheduled due date. Dr. Lansing will determine whether we need to move you to Minot. The hospital there has the closest neonatal ICU, in case we need it."

Josh heard nothing more as he descended the stairs. As a father himself, he could sympathize with Matt and Sue.

Tyler met him at the entrance to the kitchen. "Is she having the baby?"

Josh looked over Ty's head at Hilma's worried expression. "Not yet," he said. He held out his hand to the woman. "Hi. I'm Josh McBride, and you've met Tyler."

Hilma seemed to relax a little. She took his hand. "Hilma Swenson. I'm Matt's aunt." She glanced back toward the stairs. "How's she doing?"

"She's fine," Matt Connolly said as he came down the

steps. "Her doctor is on the way, but it doesn't look like the contractions are getting more frequent and there's no dilation. Gen's suspecting it's false labor, but if she's wrong, they may be able to stop it and give the baby a few more days before delivery." He turned to Josh. "Thanks for your help."

"No problem," Josh said. "I was just introducing myself to your aunt."

"Good. Well, Hilma pretty much runs the place for us, so don't get on her bad side." He winked affectionately at the woman.

"Don't you forget it," Hilma said. "Dinner's just about ready. Why don't you boys wash up? If it's okay, I'll check on Sue and see if Gen needs anything."

"Sure, go on up," Matt replied. "I don't think Gen will let her eat till the doctor's done with her, but she might want Sue to drink some water."

Hilma practically ran up the stairs.

Matt grinned. "She's kind of a mother hen, especially with the baby coming. It's been a long time since there've been children around the place."

Tyler stood at Josh's elbow. "She's nice, Dad. And she makes good cocoa. And molasses cookies."

"Molasses cookies? Before dinner?" Josh feigned a shocked expression.

Ty nodded, grinning, his earlier irritability gone. "They were great."

Josh had worried a bit about leaving Tyler while he was at work, but Hilma had clearly won him over already and done a lot to improve his mood. He had a feeling she was more than up to the task of riding herd on an active eight-year-old.

He was surprised at the mixed emotions that rose at that

thought. Ty had never really spent much time with his grandparents. Josh's own parents were deceased and since Kathy's death, Tyler's contact with her parents was limited to their infrequent returns to Seattle. Josh had gradually allowed them to grow more distant as he and Tyler traveled from place to place.

Gen came down the stairs. "I've been assigned to check on the dinner rolls in the oven while Hilma fusses over Sue." She put a hand on Matt's arm. "She's doing fine, Matt. There's no need to worry, Dr. Lansing should be here any minute."

Matt nodded. "Thanks, Gen. I know she's in good hands."

Josh watched Gen as she stepped through the door that led to the kitchen. Gen was obviously concerned about Sue. Maybe he'd been a little hasty in his comments. He'd always considered himself open-minded. He wondered if she'd taken offense at his words. She'd certainly bridled a bit.

She was probably even right about kids and childbirth. In these rural areas, it was likely that birthing was a family affair. After all, farm kids saw animals being born all the time. Maybe he could have been a little less judgmental about Gen's suggestion.

"Come on and I'll show you around," Matt said. "I think we have a couple minutes to kill before dinner."

Josh nodded, and he and Tyler followed Matt down the hall.

The doorbell rang. Gen dashed to the door as Hilma appeared at the head of the stairs. She waved the older woman back. "It's probably Dr. Lansing. I'll let her in. The rolls are done, by the way. I set them on the back of the stove to cool."

Hilma nodded and returned to the bedroom as Gen

opened the door for the doctor, a dark-haired woman in her forties. "Thanks for coming on such short notice, Carol," Gen said. "Sue's upstairs."

She led the obstetrician to the master bedroom where Hilma was busy plumping pillows and looking nervous. Sue seemed calm enough for the moment, but having Matt's aunt fluttering around couldn't be helping.

"I don't know if the chicken's ready yet, Hilma," Gen said. "But if you want to get dinner on for the guys, I'll stay here with Sue and Dr. Lansing."

Sue smiled, clearly sensing her intent. "Yes, Hilma, don't wait dinner. It'll keep them occupied. Make sure Matt eats something, too. I know he's hungry, and it'll distract him for a while."

The older woman nodded, lavender curls bobbing. "You're right. I'll take care of it, and maybe I can draft them to help with the dishes afterward. That'll keep them out of your hair."

"Good idea. Thanks." Gen watched fondly as Hilma left the room.

"That was a stroke of genius," Sue said.

Dr. Lansing grinned. "Occupying the menfolk is always a priority. Menfolk and maiden aunts. Now, Sue, how fast are the contractions coming?"

Gen watched while the doctor examined her friend and patient, paying attention but finding her thoughts drifting to Josh McBride.

She'd been surprised when he'd volunteered to carry Sue into the house. He'd made such a point of clarifying his role at the clinic, she'd have thought the last thing he'd want would be to help out in such an intimate manner.

"So, who's the hottie I saw with Matt? He's new around here." Carol Lansing's voice broke into her thoughts.

"That 'hottie' is my relief while I'm on leave," Sue replied. "And what's a married lady like you doing giving strange men the eye?"

The doctor chuckled. "I'm married, I'm not dead. I know at least one single woman in town, though, who might do more than look." She arched an eyebrow at Gen. "How 'bout it? You've been out of circulation awhile now. What do you think of this new guy?"

Gen felt her cheeks flush and suppressed a rush of annoyance at her response to the inquiry. She forced a smile. "I've already been down this line of questioning with Sue, and as I told her, I'm not in the market."

Sue snorted. "You're not even in the parking lot. When was the last time you dated?"

Gen hesitated. Honesty would prolong the conversation, but an evasive answer might provoke even more embarrassing questions. "Not since I came back to Halden," she said at last. It had actually been considerably longer, but they didn't need to know that.

"Well, I guess that's not too much of a surprise." Dr. Lansing did a final quick check of Sue's pulse. "It's not like you meet eligible men at work."

Gen laughed, despite her discomfort. "No, most of the men I meet professionally are sort of spoken for, since I'm usually delivering their wives' babies."

"Most of the men in Halden are married or elderly, anyway," Sue added.

"And the rest are either in the process of leaving or are unemployed and living in trailers on their parents' farms. That doesn't really make for good relationship prospects."

Gen shook her head. "Look you two, I know you're eager to get every single person in sight on the marital-bliss bandwagon, but I'm perfectly happy on my own."

"But you do think he's a hottie, don't you?" Sue persisted.

"He's a hottie who's going to leave town as soon as his assignment is over," Gen reminded her.

Sue apparently had no response to that, but Dr. Lansing shrugged. "Doesn't mean it can't be fun while it lasts." She patted Sue's shoulder. "Okay, go ahead and get dressed, Sue. You're not dilated or effaced, and it looks like the contractions have stopped for the moment. I'm suspecting it was Braxton Hicks. Those are normal at this stage of your pregnancy.

"I don't think there's anything to worry about," she continued, "but I want you to stay off your feet the rest of the night and make sure you're well hydrated. If contractions start again, try walking a little, drink some water, and if they don't stop, call me or Gen. If they don't recur, you can resume very light activity tomorrow, but no work, no lifting and nothing strenuous." She turned to Gen. "I know you'll be stopping by to check in on her, so keep me posted and make her behave herself."

Gen nodded. "I will. I'll let Matt know and he'll make sure she doesn't lift a finger around here."

"Perfect," Dr. Lansing said. She hugged Sue. "I'll leave you in Gen's capable hands."

Gen escorted the doctor to the front door. "Thanks for getting out here so quickly. I'll call if anything comes up."

"No problem. If no further emergencies arise, I shouldn't need to see her again till after the baby comes." The doctor glanced toward the dining room where Josh McBride was just visible at the table beyond the doorway.

"And keep in mind what I said about the hottie. You owe it to yourself."

"Uh, thanks. I'll keep it in mind." Gen didn't mention that another dead-end relationship was the last thing she needed.

Chapter Three

From his spot at the dining-room table, Josh noted the doctor's departure and Gen's cordial goodbye to her. The fact that Gen had called Dr. Lansing surprised him. In his experience with alternative-medicine adherents, he'd never noticed a willingness to work side by side with traditional practitioners.

Gen joined them at the table where a place had been reserved for her, and Hilma passed her a platter still heaped with golden fried chicken. "Well, the contractions have stopped on their own," Gen said. She placed a big drumstick on her plate and reached for a bowl of potatoes.

"Dr. Lansing wants Sue to stay off her feet tonight," she went on. "If the contractions don't start again, Matt, she can resume light activity tomorrow. Nothing strenuous, though, and make sure she drinks a lot of fluids. Dehydration can trigger contractions."

"Don't worry," Matt said. "Between Hilma and myself, she won't have a chance to do anything stressful, and we'll keep pushing the water and juice. With Josh here, she won't even need to come into the clinic, so that'll keep her away from situations where she might be tempted to lend a hand."

"I take it she was on light duty already?" Josh asked.

Gen nodded. "She was, when we could force her to take it easy. She was determined to keep working as close to her due date as possible, but there are a lot duties around a vet hospital that shouldn't be done by a pregnant woman because of potential hazards to the fetus."

"Right, exposure to gas anesthetic, contagious diseases, things like that." Josh knew the hazards to Sue were greater than just the physical exertion of a mixed large- and small-animal practice.

"She was pretty much limited to doing office exams on pets and the occasional minor surgery under injectable or local anesthetics." Matt shook his head. "She's one stubborn woman. She wanted to keep working for as long as she could, especially since she might decide to stay home once the baby comes. She wasn't going to risk the baby, though. Fortunately we have a couple of good licensed veterinary technicians at the clinic. They were able to handle a lot of the heavy stuff, between Sue's pregnancy and my back. You'll meet them tomorrow."

"I'm looking forward to it," Josh said.

Tyler reached up to tug his arm. His son looked full and sleepy, but his eyes still shone with excitement. "When will we get to see the bison?"

Hilma spoke up. "We'll get you a tour of the place tomorrow and introduce you to Tessie, our white calf. Wait, I have a picture of her." She stepped into the living room and returned a moment later with a framed photograph of a woolly, creamy-colored bison. She handed it to Tyler.

"Cool!" Tyler studied the photo, then began peppering Hilma with questions about the bison and Lilac Hills Ranch.

Matt turned to Gen. "Thanks for everything, by the way. I'd have been a wreck if you hadn't been here."

Gen shrugged. "It's my job and Sue's my best friend. You know I'd do anything for you guys." She glanced at her watch. "Speaking of my job, it's late and I have a busy day tomorrow. I'd better run."

Josh looked at his watch. It was after ten. He hadn't realized how quickly the evening had passed.

Gen rose. "Thanks for dinner, Hilma. Matt, I'll run up and check on Sue one last time, and I'll stop by tomorrow morning before my other rounds. Be sure to call me or Dr. Lansing if contractions start again and they don't go away with a little walking or fluids."

"Sure thing." Matt stood up and gave her a quick hug.

Josh rose as well and offered his hand. She took it, her fingers warm in his.

"It was nice to meet you," he said, and was amazed to find that he meant it, despite his misgivings about her. "I guess I'll see you around."

"Probably. I'll practically be living here, as often as I'll be stopping by to check on Sue." Gen glanced down at their hands.

Josh released hers, not realizing he'd still been holding it. She smiled, her expression quizzical and a little shy. She leaned across to hug Hilma, then offered a hand to Ty. "It was good to meet you, Tyler. I hope you like the bison." With that said, she dashed back up the stairs to her patient.

Hilma rose, the top of her head barely reaching Josh's chest. "Matt," she said. "Why don't you run up and see if Sue needs anything. I'll get these fellas settled for the night. Tyler is probably exhausted. The dishes can wait." She gestured to Josh and Tyler. "Come with me. I'll show you your room."

Her manner was clearly that of one used to being obeyed. Josh grinned. Matt hadn't exaggerated. For all her small stature, Hilma did indeed run things in this house. "Great, thank you," he said, and turned to his son. "Grab your duffel from the other room so we can get your pajamas."

Ty ran to follow Josh's order. When he returned, Josh took the bag, and the two McBride men followed the diminutive woman down the short hallway off the dining room that led to three spacious bedrooms. Hilma directed them into the largest. It was comfortably furnished with an antique dresser and a pair of twin beds flanking a night table. She opened two doors. The first led to the bathroom and the second to a large closet.

"This used to be the master bedroom till the upstairs was finished," she said. "We like to use it for guests, now, since it has its own bath." She handed Josh a key. "Take this in case you have to go out after hours for farm calls or emergencies. We didn't used to keep the house locked at night, but these days you can't be too careful." She walked back to the hallway. "Make yourselves at home. I hope you'll be comfortable."

She started to close the door, then hesitated and leaned back into the room. "Oh, and feel free to raid the kitchen if you get hungry."

Ty turned to Josh. "I don't think I'll be hungry again for a week."

"Me either, but thanks, Hilma. That was some dinner."

Hilma beamed with pleasure. "You're more than welcome. It's nice to cook for a big family again. 'Night, now."

His son eyed the bed and yawned, clearly against his will. "I'm not really tired yet. Can I play my Game Boy for a while?"

Josh wasn't buying it. "You can't fool me. You can barely keep your eyes open." He hefted the duffel bag onto the bed. "Get your pajamas on and brush your teeth. I'll run out and bring in the rest of our stuff."

"Aw, Dad." Ty's resistance was halfhearted, though. He was already digging through his duffel bag. Josh ruffled his son's hair and left him to his bedtime preparations.

Hilma was busy with the dishes as he passed the kitchen. He heard voices from upstairs and guessed that Matt was helping Sue settle down for the night. He stepped outside onto the broad front porch.

"Oh, hi." Gen's voice came from the corner near the rail.

"Hi. I didn't know you were still here." The porch was dark, but Josh could make out the glint of moonlight on her coppery hair.

"Just leaving, actually." She indicated the open prairie spreading out from the front of the house. "It's always pretty here. I had to stop and admire the view for a moment."

Josh followed the direction of her gesture. The prairie was beautiful at night, rolling hills picked out in a mosaic of light and shadow, and pale grasses turning silvery in the moon glow. The view on the porch wasn't bad either, he thought. Gen looked like some kind of fey, otherworldly creature, her skin pale and glimmering, her features delicate.

"I'm glad I ran into you before I left," she said, stepping closer. "I wanted to thank you."

"For what?"

"For helping with Sue. It was nice of you to volunteer to carry her inside." Her eyes were bright in the moonlight.

He shrugged. "It was nothing. I didn't want Matt to hurt his back again."

"Well, it was nice, anyway. Not everyone would have done it."

She looked away, facing the shimmering plain once more.

"You're welcome." He'd won her approval. He didn't know why that pleased him so much, but the thought sent warmth radiating through him.

They stood there in silence a moment, neither looking at the other.

"I guess I should get going," she said at last.

"Yeah, I just came out to unload the car. Ty's dead on his feet, and I'm not far behind."

"Oh, I'm keeping you up. I'm sorry." She slipped past him to the porch steps, and he noticed for the first time that she smelled of lilacs. Or maybe it was just the night breeze from the plains. Did lilacs bloom this early?

"Not at all," he started, but she was already down the steps to her car, waving as she got in. He watched as her lights disappeared down the road, then went to unpack his own vehicle.

JOSH MCBRIDE WAS clearly going to be trouble, Gen thought on the drive home from Lilac Hills.

His dismay when Tyler had asked her to ride with them and his downright disappointment when she agreed had been obvious clues that he'd taken a dislike to her from the start. Now, though, she wasn't so sure, and that bothered her even more.

Dislike she could deal with. Attraction was something else, again. And Josh McBride was attractive. As they'd stood there together on the porch in the moonlight, she'd almost been tempted....

She shook off the frightening thought, and the even scarier one that if she'd made a move, he'd have reciprocated.

I should have my head examined.

The idea of getting involved with this stranger should have sent her running for her car. Especially since his attitude toward her was questionable at best. At the clinic and on the drive to the ranch, he'd been all but hostile. That wasn't a temperament that generally appealed to her. But just now, on the porch, he'd been like a different person.

Gen shrugged. Whatever had been bothering Josh McBride, he seemed to have gotten over it. Maybe it was tension over the new assignment or fatigue from traveling. Whatever the cause, if Josh had a problem with her, she'd just stay out of his way.

If he didn't, and she'd correctly read the vibe she was getting on the porch, well, staying out of his way was an even better idea. With any luck, he'd already be at work when she came by tomorrow to visit Sue.

And afterward? Well, Halden was a small town and with the McBrides staying at Lilac Hills their paths were bound to cross, but she could handle that. She'd be polite, nothing more.

With any luck, she wouldn't need his services, either. Most of the animals she was tending were on the road to recovery and besides, Matt was still around. Sue would be on her feet in no time after having the baby, and Josh McBride would be gone.

And so would Tyler.

She considered the little boy who'd stared up at her with such wide, blue eyes, so like his father's. A twinge of sadness coursed through her at the thought of his leaving. He was so like Tommy, her younger brother, at that age. She'd practically raised Tommy and his loss, to a congenital heart defect, had been devastating. Tyler was obviously a healthy child, but she felt that he needed her care.

Your maternal instinct is showing.

Gen quashed the thought immediately. She had no maternal instinct. Nurturing instinct, yes, and that she applied to her human patients and her animals. But children?

When well-meaning friends asked her about settling down and starting a family, she always joked that her biological clock was set permanently to "snooze." It was at least partly true, but it also was simpler than explaining that her chances of having her own children were slim.

Scarring due to severe endometriosis several years earlier had left her unlikely to be able to conceive. Second and third opinions had confirmed the prognosis, and she'd accepted the probability that she'd never give birth. She loved children, but had resigned herself to the idea that a career of bringing them into the world would be enough for her.

In any case, she thought, it wasn't as if she had any prospects for marriage. She hadn't exaggerated when she'd talked about the lack of eligible men in Halden and surrounding areas. Truth was, she preferred it that way. It was safer to avoid relationships entirely than to risk the kind of involvement that might potentially lead to marriage.

It wouldn't be fair to allow herself to get close to a man who might have plans for a family. Since the status of her fertility wasn't something she felt comfortable blurting out on a first date, she found it easier to avoid dating altogether.

Whatever her feelings toward his father, though, Tyler had already won a spot in her heart. Perhaps it was his resemblance to Tommy, but maybe it was because he, like his father, was wounded in spirit. The damage was subtler than Josh's, but it was there all the same, palpable to her healer's senses.

The recognition saddened her. This was no injured animal she could bandage, feed and comfort, then return to the wild. Both McBrides were injured in a way she had no power to cure, no matter how strong her nurturing instinct.

Frustration weighing on her, she turned her compact wagon down the long driveway and soon was in sight of her house. The view buoyed her spirits as it always did after a long or difficult day. Here at least was something she could do, a difference she could make. Here she was needed and even loved.

She turned the key in the door, stepped inside and braced for the impact she knew was coming. Right on schedule, a small, black-and-white cat leaped to her shoulder from atop a bookcase near the door. He meowed once, loudly, in her face, then nuzzled her cheek, purring. Another cat, a plump yellow longhair, twined itself around her ankles, mewing for attention.

The rest of the house seemed to awaken at the cats' welcome. Whistles, croaks and strange rustling sounds came from the back rooms.

"Okay, guys, I'm home. Give me a minute." Gen crouched carefully to drop her purse and medical kit by the door as the cat on her shoulder dug claws in to steady itself. She winced. "Ouch. You're due for a trim, Scotty." She pried the cat loose and plopped him on the floor next to his longhaired companion, then followed as they led the way to the kitchen.

Scotty, the Cling-on cat, and Simba, the Not-Terribly-

Bright, flowed around her feet as she filled their dishes. Soon they were busy eating, Scotty pawing one kibble at a time from his dish with dainty precision, then scarfing it off the floor, while Simba buried his face in his dish and wolfed down the triangular bits, purring and crunching at the same time.

With the cats occupied, Gen made her way to her makeshift infirmary to check on her nonhuman patients. Despite the hard winter, she'd seen few animals suffering from exposure, frostbite or starvation, and her hospital "beds" were mostly unoccupied. It was only the end of February, though, and the season was by no means over. Sometimes March and April could be the harshest months for local wildlife.

The young rabbit in the first cage had come out the worse from an encounter with some kind of predator, probably a hawk. The laceration across his shoulder was healing nicely, however, and he'd probably be ready for release in another week or two.

She filled his dish with food and offered carrot and apple chunks. After days of handling, the rabbit was becoming easier to work with, curiosity replacing fearfulness. Gen resisted the urge to coax the animal to her and pet it, though she knew she could. Her intent wasn't to tame these animals, but to rehabilitate them for release. Turning wildlife into pets would benefit neither them nor her. And Scotty and Simba would be mightily put out if strange animals started hanging around after their injuries were healed.

A low croak shook her from her reverie. She turned toward the white pelican staring at her from a wire pen that occupied almost half the room. The bird, though a juvenile by the dusky shade of its bill, was nearly full-grown at almost five feet long from bill to tail. Standing between its nesting box and the small blue kiddie pool Gen had provided for exercise, it glared at her and croaked again.

Gen laughed. "Stay calm. It's coming."

The pelican's protests became more urgent and it plucked at the wire of the pen with its bill as Gen crossed to the little refrigerator, opened it and took out a tray of small, glistening fish.

She smiled at the bird. "This what you're looking for?"

She unlatched the pen and the huge bird waddled out, one wing tucked against its side. Struck by a car, the pelican, whose presence seemed incongruous in landlocked North Dakota but was actually quite common, had been unable to migrate. Its broken wing was healing well, though. Gen had recently taken the bandages off and set up the pool for physical therapy. Later in the spring, when the pelicans returned, the bird would probably be strong enough to rejoin its flock.

Gen tossed a fish and the bird snatched it in midair, gulping greedily. After several more, it seemed sated and returned to its pen, climbing into the pool to splash noisily.

Gen shook her head. "Keep it up," she said indulgently. "There's a square foot of floor you haven't soaked yet."

Sighing, she reached for her mop and cleaning supplies, grateful, again, that she'd decided not to carpet this room. She really didn't mind cleaning up after her charges, though. Before long, they would be healthy, strong and ready to return to the wild, and she would have gotten them there.

If only there were some way she could provide the same mending to the McBride men.

Chapter Four

"I like the ranch, Dad. It's neater than any place we've ever stayed." Tyler shoved back the covers of the twin bed, climbed between the sheets and sat cross-legged.

"I'm glad you like it." Josh stood beside his own bed, pulling travel-wrinkled clothes from their bags. "It is a neat ranch."

"Yeah. Dinner was real good, too."

"It sure was," Josh agreed. "We don't get meals like that very often." He crossed to the small closet with a bundle of clothes and began to hang them on the wire hangers inside. "What did you like best?"

"Dessert. I haven't had chocolate cake in a long time."

"Not since your birthday."

"That was at a restaurant, so it doesn't count," Ty said. "It only counts if someone makes it and I get the whole cake."

"I see." Josh nodded, trying not to wince at the implication. "I didn't know those were the rules. Besides, you don't really get the whole cake. You have to share."

Tyler shrugged and lay down. "Yeah, but I can have more tomorrow. Hilma said so."

"She did, huh? Well, that settles it, then." After experiencing Hilma's cooking, Josh knew it wouldn't do to flout her wishes. He pulled the last items from his suitcase, closed it and set it on the floor. "I'm a big fan of chocolate cake myself."

"It's my favorite. Dad, do you like Gen?"

Tyler's change of subject caught Josh flat-footed. He looked down at his son. Ty gazed back at him, a slight frown on his freckled face.

Josh sat on the edge of the bed and stalled for time, smoothing the covers up around the neck of Tyler's SpongeBob Squarepants pajamas. "I just met her, Ty," he said casually. "I really don't know her well enough to know if I like her or not."

"I just met her today, too, and I like her. She's nice." Ty rolled onto his side, yawned and scrunched up the covers beside him to form a small bundle he could cuddle.

The little-boy gesture brought a sudden sting to Josh's eyes. Until recently, Ty had had a bear, Mr. Pockets, a scruffy, brown, worn teddy. Mr. Pockets had been left behind on one of their assignments, and although the motel where they'd stayed had sent him along afterward, he'd never caught up with his boy. Josh had offered to buy his son a new bear, but Ty had refused, saying that at eight years old he was much too grown-up to sleep with stuffed animals.

"She's real pretty, isn't she?"

Josh swallowed hard. "Um, yeah, I guess so. I mean, she's not bad. Kind of short." He hoped he sounded nonchalant. He certainly didn't feel it. Gen *was* pretty. More than pretty. He'd have to be blind not to notice, no matter how strong his aversion to her work.

Tyler giggled. "No, Dad, not Gen. Tessie, the bison. Her picture was pretty. I can't wait to see her for real."

Josh released a breath he hadn't realized he'd been holding as relief that was blended with embarrassment washed over him. "Oh. Yeah. Tessie's beautiful. I've never seen a more beautiful animal."

Ty snorted. "Eew, you really do think Gen's pretty, don't you, Dad?"

Josh suppressed the urge to protest. That would only settle the matter more firmly in his son's mind. He reached across and switched off the bedside lamp. "I think it's past your bedtime. It's been a busy day and we've got to get you enrolled in school tomorrow." Maybe Ty would forget this conversation by morning. Josh hoped so. He kissed his son on the cheek and forehead, then walked to the door.

"Dad?"

"What?" Josh paused and turned back.

"It's okay. I won't tell Gen you think she's pretty."

Josh shook his head and pulled the door closed behind him, then returned to the kitchen, although he wanted nothing more than to call it a day. Tomorrow he'd start at the Halden clinic, and he wanted to be well rested. A farm practice could be challenge enough without sleep deprivation.

He had to give the appearance of being sociable, though. The residents of Lilac Hills Ranch were providing him and Tyler with room and board at no cost. Avoiding their company would make him seem like an ingrate, or worse, a prima donna.

When he reached the kitchen, Hilma was drying the last of the dinner dishes. "Have a seat in the living room, Josh. I've got apple pie and decaf coffee."

Josh did as he was told, settling onto the comfortable flower-print sofa.

Matt was sprawled in a battered recliner, reading a newspaper. "Got Tyler all settled?" He laid his paper aside. "Bet he was asleep before his head hit the pillow."

Josh smiled. "Well, not quite." He knew it would be a while before his excited son got to sleep.

Matt nodded. "New surroundings to get used to. It must be hard on a kid."

"Yeah, well, he's been through it before. He adjusts pretty quickly."

"Has to, I guess, with all that moving around," Hilma responded as she came in carrying a tray laden with cups of steaming coffee and slices of pie. "Poor little guy. He was on his last legs."

Josh flinched. The older woman probably hadn't meant it as a criticism, but he felt an unfamiliar twinge of guilt, nonetheless. "He'll get a good night's sleep tonight. The room's great, by the way. Thanks again for letting us stay."

Hilma set the tray on the coffee table and accepted the change of subject without comment. "Oh, it's no problem at all. We enjoy having you and appreciate you filling in for Sue."

She handed Josh a dessert plate covered with a huge slab of apple pie and a mound of vanilla ice cream, then placed a cup of coffee before him. "I have cream and sugar, if you need them."

"No, black's fine." Josh regarded the plate of pie with something akin to awe. "I hope I can do this justice. I'm still full from dinner, not to mention chocolate cake."

Hilma grinned, her blue eyes twinkling. "We don't usually have two desserts, but I thought Tyler might like the cake. Anyway, you'll manage. You look like you could do with a little fattening up." She turned to Matt. "Was Sue sleepy? She didn't have supper. If she's awake, I'll take her some pie, or maybe heat up some chicken and potatoes."

Matt shook his head. "She was pretty wiped out and said she was going right to sleep."

"That's probably best." Hilma handed him a plate of pie. "She should sleep while she can. She's got about eighteen years of sleepless nights ahead of her."

"My mother-in-law said the same thing to me when Tyler was born." Josh smiled at the memory. "Scary thing is, it's true." He tasted the pie. It was delicious and he told Hilma so.

"Glad you like it." Hilma blushed to the gray roots of her lavender hair.

"Hilma's a fantastic cook," Matt said. "She keeps me in shape." He patted his solid middle, then took a sip of his coffee. "Decaf, bleh. Hardly worth it."

Hilma snorted. "You know it's not that bad, and it's just temporary. Once the baby's born, I'll switch back to regular."

"She's got us all on the maternity diet," Matt explained. "No caffeine, extra calcium. I swear I'm eating for two myself."

Hilma laughed. "I'm just trying to make it easier for Sue. Besides, you've been eating for two as long as I've known you. You're just lucky you've got the Connolly metabolism or you'd be big as a house." She turned to Josh. "If you're not too tired, how about a game of cards? Ever play Norwegian Blitz?"

Josh shook his head. "Never even heard of it."

She rose. "Come on then. We'll teach you. We'll use the kitchen table. How do you feel about gambling?"

THREE HOURS and numerous rounds of Norwegian Blitz later, Josh lay in the second twin bed staring at the ceiling as Tyler snored softly across from him.

During the game, Matt and Hilma had treated him like one of the family, teasing him when he handed over a card someone else needed, playfully threatening revenge when he won a hand.

They were great people and he liked them a lot. Despite his best intentions, he found himself enjoying their camaraderie. The realization surprised him.

He'd had no intention of getting close to them, but after just a few hours, he was already settling in and becoming comfortable with them. Maybe it was because they were used to taking in strays, he thought, considering the way they'd apparently adopted Gen as one of their own. For the first time in a long time, the idea of becoming part of a family again didn't disturb him.

He thought back to the guilt he'd felt at Hilma's comment. For a long time after Kathy's death, Josh had made a point of keeping Ty and himself isolated during his assignments. They'd lived out of motels, eaten in fast-food joints and diners, and kept social contact with the locals to a minimum. Josh was self-aware enough to know it was his way of avoiding thinking about home and family, about what he'd lost.

That had been fine when Ty was small, but now his son was reaching the age where friends and social interactions were important. Although he always seemed to adapt to being uprooted every few weeks and dragged to another job in a different town, the transition was taking longer each time. Tyler was having more trouble in school, acting more rebellious.

Josh suddenly remembered long-buried feelings of resentment. He'd hated leaving friends and familiar surroundings, hated living as if his family was in the witness-protection program. Funny, he hadn't thought about that in a long time.

Maybe he'd done Tyler a disservice by preventing attachments. If he kept it up, eventually Ty would learn to keep people at arm's length, like Josh did, and moving away would get easier.

Did he really want that? Josh kept telling himself that he'd turned out fine, but was it fair to inflict the same life on his son?

Surely, as long as they were together, that was all that mattered. Tyler would be fine. In any case, Josh wasn't at all sure he was ready to rejoin the human race. The habits of the past died hard.

Josh groaned and rolled over in the small bed, burying his face in his pillow as if that would drown out the nagging thoughts. It didn't.

The image of Gen Halvorson sprang forcibly to mind. Josh could picture that radiant smile of hers and almost hear her laughter as she'd chatted with Ty on the drive over. He recalled how she'd looked on the porch, the moonlight turning her pale skin to silver.

Shoving the image from his mind, he forced himself to concentrate on something else, anything else. He'd been there, done that, and knew from experience the pain that could follow.

TY WOKE EARLY the next morning. Josh could feel his son's stare even with his eyes closed and reluctantly opened them. Ty sat on his own bed grinning as Josh glanced at the clock and groaned. What kind of sixth sense did parents have, Josh wondered, that made them aware of their kid's every move?

He sighed with resignation and sat up, surprised he'd slept as well as he did considering the swirl of thoughts occupying his brain the night before.

"Can we go see Tessie?" Tyler was wasting no time this morning.

"It's six-thirty, buddy. I think we'd best wait till the rest of the house is up."

Ty hopped off the bed, managing to miss the throw rug so his bare feet slapped loudly on the hardwood floor.

Josh caught his son by the shoulder, preempting his headlong flight across the room and out the door. "That doesn't mean it's your job to wake the rest of the house. Get dressed, but keep the noise down."

Ty did his best, meaning the noise was only a dull roar. Josh could hear voices down the hall, though, and knew someone else rose early at Lilac Hills. At least Ty wouldn't be responsible for completely changing their schedules.

"SO, DID I HEAR that you'd like to see Tessie?" Hilma asked Tyler over a heaping plate of pancakes and bacon.

"Yeah!" the boy said eagerly, then glanced at his father. "I mean, yes, ma'am. Can we go now?"

"Soon as breakfast is over, if it's okay with your dad?" The older woman glanced at Josh for approval.

Josh nodded. "Sure. I'd like to see her myself."

Gen came into the kitchen with Matt. Josh hadn't realized she was already at the ranch.

"Everything looks good," she was saying. "I think she'll make it to full term with no problem. Keep her resting as much as possible and don't let her exert herself. I'll stop back over tomorrow, but don't hesitate to call if you need me."

Matt nodded. "Don't worry, I will. Thanks."

Gen's attention settled on Josh and she gave a shy smile. "Morning. I see you're getting an early start."

Josh nodded toward Ty. "Couldn't keep the kid in bed any longer."

Tyler spoke up. "Hi, Gen. Do you want to come with us to see Tessie? We're going as soon as we're done." He chomped a crisp slice of bacon and chewed it quickly.

His invitation startled Josh, but he knew he shouldn't be surprised. Ty was obviously already taken with Gen. That was understandable. Nonetheless, Josh wished his son hadn't been so quick to invite her. After last night, he'd feel more comfortable putting a little distance between them.

Gen glanced at Josh briefly, her expression unreadable, then smiled down at Tyler. "Why yes, thank you for asking, Tyler. I'd like that."

Ty pumped his fist. "Yes! I can't wait to see Tessie. How old is she?"

"She was born late last spring," Hilma said. "Hundreds of people have come to visit her."

"I understand white bison are rare," Josh said.

Matt nodded. "Especially the ones like Tessie that aren't albino. They're so rare that scientists aren't even sure of the statistics. They think the odds of a white bison birth are anywhere from one in a million to one in forty million."

"Is that why so many people visit her?" Ty asked.

"That and because she's a sacred animal to the Sioux," Matt replied. "I'll come along and you can help me feed her, Ty."

"Cool!"

Matt led the way outside with Hilma, while Josh brought up the rear. Gen and Tyler walked together between them, talking animatedly. In contrast to the loose, stretchy outfit she'd had on for her class last night, this morning Gen wore jeans and a woolly turtleneck under a well-worn leather jacket.

Josh could make out the gentle swell of her hips and firm curve of her bottom through the denim. He blinked and looked away abruptly, annoyed at himself, to focus once more on the ranch grounds.

The ranch had a large barn, a couple smaller outbuildings, a corral and loafing shed. Hilma led them to the corral first and helped Tyler up onto the railing.

"This is where Matt and Sue first met," she said. She glanced between Josh and Gen, her eyes twinkling. "We had Tessie's mama in here then. She was pregnant with Tessie, and we had to keep an eye on her."

Gen narrowed her eyes at the older woman. What exactly was she hinting at? If Hilma had matchmaking designs on her and Josh McBride, she was in for a big letdown. Aside from her own medical issues, Gen didn't intend to let herself get involved with a man who'd be moving on when Sue's leave was over in six or eight weeks. Besides, every bit of intuition she had told her a relationship was the last thing Josh McBride wanted.

"Where is Tessie's mom now?" Tyler asked.

"She's out on the range with the rest of the herd. We're hoping she'll have another calf this season."

"Can we go out and see the herd?" Tyler wanted to know.

"We won't have time this morning since Josh and I have to get to the clinic," Matt replied. "Maybe if we have a light load at work this afternoon, your dad can hold down the fort while I take you out to see them."

"Are they dangerous?" Josh asked.

His voice was steady, but Gen could feel concern behind his words. She couldn't blame him for not wanting his son exposed to anything risky.

"Well, I wouldn't recommend walking through the herd," Matt replied. "We'll be perfectly safe in the truck, though. They're used to it and know it's no threat to them."

"Tessie's mother is pretty tame, too," Gen added. "She was hand-reared, and sometimes she comes up to the truck for a head-scratching."

"Wow! Can I go, Dad? I promise I'll be good." Tyler looked appealingly at his father.

Josh frowned. "I don't know. I don't think you should impose on Matt."

Matt spoke up. "It's no imposition. I'm happy to show him the herd."

"Neat! Will you be here, Gen?" Tyler turned to her. "I'd like you to come, too."

"I think I'm free this afternoon, but…" Gen hesitated, glancing at Josh. She didn't want to intrude, especially since Josh seemed to be trying to dissuade his son from going.

"Tyler, I don't think you need to rope Gen into this," Josh said. "She's probably busy enough with her own work."

Gen noted the pointed way he looked at her, but spoke without thinking. "I really don't mind, Josh. I'd be happy to go with Matt and Tyler."

Josh gave a short sigh of resignation, clearly unable to fight all of them. "Okay, well, I guess if you both don't mind…"

"Yeah," Tyler said. "Now let's go see Tessie."

"She's in the barn." Matt led the way across the dusty yard.

The morning sun was bright and the day was rapidly growing warmer. The sunshine was deceptive, though, Josh realized, as he noticed that the small puddles on the ground were icy. Well, it was still February, after all. That was hardly spring in the Dakotas.

He watched Tyler for signs of chill, feeling guilty for not making his son grab a heavier jacket before coming out. Of course, Ty would have balked at wearing anything warmer than his hooded sweatshirt jacket, anyway. He never seemed to feel the cold and Josh knew he was falling into the old parental habit of making his child dress warmly when he, himself, felt cold.

He's fine, worrywart.

The voice in his head was Kathy's, as much as his own. She'd been an amazingly relaxed mother with her only son, never fanatical over germs or chilly weather, and Tyler had thrived under her care.

"Are you cold, Tyler?" Gen Halvorson asked, as though she'd read Josh's thoughts.

"No." The boy shook his head and Gen, taking him at his word, didn't press like most adults would have. He stopped beside Matt and wrinkled his nose as the vet slid open the broad barn door. "Wow, it smells cow-y."

Hilma laughed. "Yep, buffalo smell a lot like cows. Pretty stinky, huh?"

Tyler nodded. "It's a different kind of stinky. Sorta like old hay. Not really bad stinky."

"Good stinky, eh?" Matt asked. He glanced over his shoulder at Josh. "I think this boy's born to be a rancher."

"Or a cowboy," Tyler said, warming to the idea. "Do they still have cowboys?"

"Sure they do," Hilma replied. "Not on a small place like

this, of course, but some big ranches, especially in the Southwest, still have them."

"Do they wear ten-gallon hats and carry pistols?"

"Yes on the hats—well, Stetsons or Resistols, anyway, but no on the pistols," Josh said.

"Darn." Sincere regret tinged the boy's voice.

That Tyler was taking such an interest pleased and surprised Josh. Lately, it seemed he was eight years old going on sixteen, demonstrating a surliness that would make a teenager proud.

When he wanted to, anyway. Sometimes, like today, he could be outgoing and interested, his usual bright and imaginative self. Josh hoped it would continue once he was enrolled in school.

Matt stopped before a stall that took up nearly a quarter of the barn. It was decorated with Native American shields and symbols, and an arch rose above it proclaiming *PtesanWi* in huge, gilt letters.

"This is PtesanWi," he said. "That's the Lakota Sioux name for White Buffalo Woman, the spirit woman who brought the bison to the Sioux people. We call her Tessie for short."

The single occupant of the stall snuffled at the sound of voices, raising a woolly head and ambling to the gate as though pleased to have visitors.

Tessie was large for a yearling calf. Josh had seen images of white buffalo in paintings and movies, stark, snowy white, like quadruped clouds. Surely no bison could be that white, that clean.

Tessie wasn't cloud-white, or even snowy. Her shade was softer, the color of fresh-skimmed cream, and she was surprisingly clean. He stretched out a hand, without conscious thought, then stopped as he realized what he was doing and glanced at Matt. "Can I touch her?"

The vet nodded. "She was hand-raised. She's very gentle, and loves people, which is a good thing, considering how many come to see her. She likes to be scratched behind the ears. Any bison can be unpredictable, though, even if it's only because they don't know their own strength."

Josh nodded. He wouldn't want to risk sharing a pen with Tessie, hand-reared or not. Though not yet full grown, she weighed several hundred pounds, enough to affectionately crush a person without realizing she was hurting him. He reached over the gate and the huge animal sidled up against the fence to permit his touch.

Josh ran his hand up the densely furred forehead and Tessie lowered her head so he could reach her ears. "She feels so clean. I wouldn't have expected that of a bison."

"Well, she's not quite that tidy naturally," Hilma said. "We bathe her once a week or so, depending on the weather."

"You bathe her?" Josh tried to picture that. It must be like washing a hairy car.

Hilma nodded. "She likes to play in water. Has ever since she was a baby. Now we just fasten a halter to her to keep her in one place, soak her down, shampoo and rinse. Of course, whoever bathes her usually gets a pretty good washing themselves."

"I don't doubt it."

With her head down for ear scratching, Tessie had her nose level with Tyler's chest and the boy touched it tentatively through the railing.

Tessie gave a loud snort. Tyler jumped back with a yelp.

Matt laughed. "She's just telling your dad she likes having her ears scratched." He coaxed Tyler back to the rail. "See." He reached in to pat her muzzle and she swiped his hand with a long tongue.

Tyler followed Matt's lead, petting the animal again, and was rewarded with a soggy slurp. He grimaced. "Eew, buffalo spit." He didn't seem the least perturbed by it, though.

Too short to reach the bison over the gate, Gen climbed up on the railing to scratch Tessie's head. She stood next to Josh stroking one woolly ear while he scratched the other.

He had thought he'd feel awkward so close to her, especially after last night. But standing together, concentrating on the animal, felt surprisingly normal. If one could feel normal standing in a barn, petting a white buffalo.

The bison raised her head, eyed Gen, and then, as if recognizing her, danced eagerly toward her, moving with surprising speed for such a big animal. Gen stretched over the railing to wrap her arms around the top of Tessie's head, below the growing horns, and scratch behind both ears at once.

Josh could see the animal lean into the railing as though surrendering wholeheartedly to the caress.

"Wow, she really likes you." The admiration in Tyler's voice was undisguised.

"Animals love Gen," Hilma said. "I've never seen anything like it."

Animals and children, Josh thought, noting Tyler's fond expression. That combination could prove dangerous for a man determined to maintain his distance.

Chapter Five

They returned to the house where, after a last check on Sue, Gen left the ranch for her other calls. Josh saw the disappointment in Tyler's eyes as he watched her leave and was surprised at his own feelings of regret. He told himself it was for Ty's sake, but a voice inside wanted to argue and he found himself thinking back to his view of her curved derriere as she'd walked ahead of him to the barn. He shook off the thought, annoyed at himself, and went to find Matt, anxious for a distraction.

"I'm getting ready to head into town," Matt said as Josh approached. "Did you want to take Tyler up to the school and get him registered this morning?"

Josh nodded. "Yeah, the sooner he's settled the better."

"Aw, Dad, do I have to?" Ty glanced out at the barn, his expression wistful. "I could stay here and help with the bison."

Josh tousled his son's sandy hair. "Sorry, buddy. School first, then animals. That's the rule."

"Oh, fine." Ty looked dejected, but only for a moment. This wasn't a battle he expected to win, anyway.

Matt laughed. "We'll be happy to put you to work after school, Ty. There's plenty around here to keep you busy."

To Josh he said, "I'll drive on in, then. The school is a couple blocks beyond the clinic as you enter Halden. Come on over once you're done. There's an employee lot behind the building where you can park." He pulled on a weather-beaten coat and called up the stairs to Sue, "I'm out of here, hon. I'll have my cell phone on if you need anything."

"Bye, sweetie," Sue called back. "Have a good day."

Matt gave Josh and Ty a quick wave, then left the house. Josh felt a stab of envy at the obvious and easy affection between Matt and Sue. Would he ever be ready for that kind of relationship?

As SHE DROVE to her next appointment, Gen wanted to smack herself in the forehead. What had she done, accepting Tyler's invitation again? She liked the little boy and found it impossible to say no to him, but by doing so she found herself at odds with his father. She suspected that Josh McBride was less than thrilled at her offer to accompany his son to see the bison. She'd known what his response would be, but she'd gone ahead and said yes anyway. What must Josh be thinking?

He probably thought she was chasing him. Matt and Sue had made it clear when he arrived that she was single, and to most men, that would imply she was looking. If the last thing she needed was a relationship, the next-to-last thing was some man who thought she was looking for one.

She groaned aloud. She needed to keep her distance, from both Tyler and his father. That was going to be hard with daily visits to Lilac Hills to check on Sue.

At least Josh wouldn't be with them this afternoon when she went out to see the herd with Tyler and Matt. Maybe she could plan her trips to the ranch for later in the day to ensure she arrived after Josh left for work. It would mean reorganizing her schedule. Since the ranch was closest to her home and most of her patients lived on the other side of Lilac Hills, nearer to town, she usually stopped to see Sue first.

Gen shook her head. No, she had to be grown-up about this. She couldn't schedule her whole life around avoiding Josh McBride. She could, however, gently decline any more of Tyler's invitations. Before long Josh would be gone and the matter would have taken care of itself.

The thought of Josh's eventual departure didn't give her the sense of relief she'd expected, but she refused to analyze it further. She turned her car in at her next patient's driveway and forced her mind back to her job.

JOSH LEFT the school in Halden, a low-slung brick building with a gym/auditorium at one end, comfortable that his son was in good hands. The school was small, combining both elementary and junior-high classes, and was attended by children from town and from the farms and ranches in the area. High-schoolers were bused to the neighboring town of Rorvik for their classes. Ty's young teacher, a Mrs. Osborne, seemed energetic and attentive, and his son had warmed to her on the spot.

First Gen and now Mrs. Osborne, Josh thought. He'd never realized before how much his son missed the presence of a woman in his life. The recognition brought back another twinge of doubt about uprooting Tyler so frequently.

He recalled his walk with Tyler to the school office, noting that his son had made a point of letting go of Josh's hand as they entered the building. Ty was growing up. At the advanced age of eight, he was probably embarrassed to be seen holding his daddy's hand in public. Josh suspected that before long, his mere presence would be an embarrassment to his son. He welcomed his son's independence, even as a pang of sadness squeezed his heart.

He found the veterinary clinic again easily and pulled in to the employee lot. The clinic had a back door, presumably the employee entrance. Somehow barging in didn't feel right, so he knocked.

Matt opened the door, grinning. "You made it! Got Tyler enrolled, then?"

"He's all set," Josh replied. "He gets out at three. There's a school-bus stop near Lilac Hills, so he'll catch the bus back there most days, but today he'll just come back here."

"Great. We have a light schedule this afternoon, so if you want to keep an eye on things till closing, I'll take him to see the herd once school's out."

Josh nodded. "Sounds good, thanks. I know he'll enjoy that."

Matt introduced Josh to the clinic staff, which consisted of Elaine, the receptionist, a no-nonsense lady who was probably in her sixties, if her cap of iron-gray curls was any indication, and two veterinary technicians, Beth and Terry. The techs were both twentysomething, blond and similar enough in appearance that Josh had to ask if they were related.

Beth, the taller of the two, giggled. "We're cousins."

Terry nodded. "Double cousins. My mom's sister married my dad's brother. It was a double wedding."

"And we were born just a couple months apart," Beth added. "So we're more like sisters than cousins."

"Beth and Terry do a lot of the well-animal office calls," Matt said. "Vaccinations, mostly. If an animal needs an exam or if they notice anything unusual, they'll call one of us in. They also prep for and assist in surgery, do routine teeth-cleanings, treat hospitalized patients, do any lab work that we don't send out and sometimes assist on farm calls. They're both great technicians, the clients love them and they free us up for the heavy-duty stuff."

The young women blushed at his praise.

"Come on," he continued. "I'll give you a tour of the place."

As Josh had noted when he arrived during Gen's class, the clinic was modern and well-appointed. The main floor of the building, once a private home, comprised a waiting area and front office, two exam rooms, a cozy employee lounge, and a shared office for the veterinarians. Downstairs, in what had been the basement, were a large treatment area, a surgical suite, kennels and wards for patients. Matt showed Josh around, then they returned to the office where he invited Josh to make himself at home at Sue's desk.

He'd just stowed his belongings when Elaine came to the door of the office.

"Mrs. Gentry is here with Greta for an ear exam." She peered meaningfully at Josh over a thick file folder.

He rose, taking the hint. "I guess this one's mine."

Matt nodded. "Go for it. Be careful, though—she's a snappy cocker spaniel with chronic otitis."

Josh laughed. "Well, if I'm going to get bitten, I might as well get it over with the first day." He took the folder from Elaine, noting the word *Caution* printed in red marker at the top of the dog's chart, and headed for the exam room with Beth close behind.

As soon as he entered the room, he smelled the distinctive waxy, wet-dog aroma of inflamed cocker spaniel ears and expected the worst. Greta, however, was in a docile mood, or maybe her ear infection hadn't progressed to the point of making her cranky. The small black dog wagged her stumpy tail as he spoke calming words to her, and she allowed Beth to restrain her for her exam without resistance.

Josh held out his hand to Mrs. Gentry, a diminutive, white-haired lady. "How do you do, Mrs. Gentry? I'm Dr. McBride. I'm filling in while Dr. Connolly is out on leave."

"How do you do, Doctor?" The woman took his hand, her grip strong despite the fragile look of her thin, blue-veined hands. "Welcome to Halden."

"Thank you. Looks like Greta here has some problems with her ears."

The owner nodded. "Yes, she always has infections, poor baby." She reached past Beth to pat the spaniel's silky head. "There, there, honey. The nice doctor will fix you right up."

Josh cleaned and treated both ears, then wrote a prescription for an ear ointment. "I'm going to try her on a different medication than she's had before. She might have less resistance to it. Be sure to apply it in the ear canal twice a day."

Mrs. Gentry winced. "She hates having her ears messed with, Doctor."

"I know, but if you don't treat them now, they'll get worse and that'll make treatment even more difficult." He handed her the prescription slip.

The woman nodded. "I'll try. Maybe my son can come over and help hold her."

"That's a good idea." He made a few notes in Greta's chart, then handed the file to Beth. "I'd like to see her back in a week. Elaine will set you up with an appointment."

"Thank you, Doctor." Mrs. Gentry snapped on Greta's leash and let Beth lower the dog to the floor, then she paused to shake Josh's hand once more. "I'm glad Dr. Connolly has such a nice young man helping out. I'll see you next week."

"Thank you, Mrs. Gentry." The woman's kind words, coupled with Greta's forbearance, gave him a warm glow and a feeling of goodwill toward potentially snappy spaniels everywhere. The morning was shaping up well.

It didn't last. His next patient was a long-haired calico cat with a bite wound over her hip. Her owner, a stressed-looking young mother who'd left two small children in the waiting room, much to Elaine's displeasure, had placed the cat's plastic carrier on the exam table and seemed disinclined to remove her for his examination. The cat, Bubbles, crouched at the back of the box, a tricolored ball of hissing, yowling fluff.

Josh introduced himself to the owner. "Want to get her out?" he suggested.

The woman shook her head. "Not hardly. She'll claw me to pieces. She's grouchy enough when she's not hurt. I could barely get her in the carrier."

Great. Josh knew his day had gotten off to too easy a start. "Okay, I'll give it a try."

He opened the metal door of the box. A loud hiss like that of a rattlesnake sounded and a white paw flashed toward his hand. The talonlike claw connected with the back of his thumb, leaving a stripe across the knuckle that immediately welled with blood.

Josh bit back a curse and forced a smile at the owner, whose expression said she'd told him so. "Looks like we'll have to try something else. Just a sec," he excused himself, and stepped into the hall, grabbing a tissue to blot his wound.

Matt was passing on his way to the second exam room. He glanced at Josh's bloody thumb. "Calico, huh? Psychos, all of 'em." He reached into a hall cabinet and pulled out a pair of rawhide gloves. "Give these a try." He handed them to Josh, then pressed a button on the intercom and called down to the lounge area, "Terry, Beth, we need a hand here if either of you are free."

Terry stepped into the hall and looked at Josh's hand. "Happy to help. Calico, huh?"

Josh nodded. "She has a bite wound. Doesn't want to leave the carrier."

Terry took a pair of gloves and slipped them on. "Do you want sedation?"

"No, let's see what we're dealing with first. If it's not abscessed yet I'd prefer not to put her under."

He led the way back into the room and held the box while Terry reached slowly inside with one armored hand. The owner had taken a seat to watch the proceedings from a safe distance.

Bubbles growled, a low throaty whine, then the box began to thrash wildly.

"Got her," Terry said. "Just a minute." She pulled her gloved hand out of the carrier. Bubbles clung to it by her teeth and four sets of bared claws. Terry kept pressure on the animal so she couldn't let go and make a run for it, then shifted the cat and took hold of her by the scruff of the neck.

Bubbles seemed unwilling to release her grip on the glove, gnawing it angrily as she continued to growl. She was out of the carrier and restrained, though, so Josh found the wound with no further trouble. He shaved the long hair around the site and cleaned it. "Is this from another cat?" he asked the owner.

The woman nodded. "She's pretty territorial. Attacks any other cat that comes in the yard."

Imagine that, Josh thought. "Well, it's not abscessed, only inflamed at this point. We'll start her on antibiotics and see if we can keep it from getting worse." He frowned. Treating the cat at home was likely to be as difficult as doing it here. "Can you give her pills?"

"No, but she likes that pink liquid stuff."

"She likes it?" In Josh's experience, cats rarely liked the bubble-gum-flavored oral antibiotic that was originally a pediatric medication, but who was he to argue?

"Okay, we'll go with that, then." He made notes in the chart, then turned to Terry. "Hold her a couple minutes longer. I'll start her with an injection and get her meds for home."

The cat took the antibiotic injection with relative grace, still chewing on Terry's gloved hand, and Josh handed the owner a labeled bottle of antibiotic. "Keep her on that till it's gone, and bring her back if you see any swelling or drainage around the bite."

"I will. Thanks, Doctor." Apparently more in the mood to participate now, she held the carrier close to the cat as Terry released her grip. Bubbles disengaged her fangs from the rawhide glove and darted back into the relative safety of her cage, whirling to face her tormentors while spitting a warning lest they try to remove her again.

Josh looked at his thumb. The deep scratch stung and was starting to get puffy and red. Oh well, he thought, at least she hadn't bitten him. Cat bites were notorious for getting infected, while a scratch was generally a minor annoyance at most. He scrubbed his hands with antiseptic soap, dabbed on some antibiotic ointment and bandaged the wound, then checked with Elaine for his next appointment.

GEN SAT in the truck next to Matt while Tyler called "Shotgun," and claimed the window seat. Josh had been with a patient when she stopped by the clinic to meet Matt and Tyler for their bison-viewing trip, so she'd missed seeing him.

Relief and disappointment mingled and she stifled a sigh. This was far too confusing. Tyler was happy to see her, though, and she took comfort in that.

"I'm glad you didn't have to work this afternoon, Gen," he said.

"Me, too, Tyler. I don't get to see the bison often enough. I'm glad I didn't have to miss the tour."

"It might be a short tour, unfortunately," Matt said. "I think we're about to get a storm."

The sky, sunny early in the day, had turned gray and threatening. Gen noticed that a few flakes of snow had started to filter down, ample evidence that, although it was nearly March, the North Dakota winter was not yet ready to release its hold on the plains.

"Do you think it'll snow hard?" Tyler asked, excitement in his voice. "Maybe they'll close the school."

Matt laughed. "You just started. Do you want a snow day already?"

"Sure," the boy replied. "I want to build snowmen."

"I don't think it'll snow hard enough for that," Gen said. The forecasts weren't calling for much more than a dusting. She was glad of that. Trying to reach her patients in a heavy snowstorm could be a nightmare.

They arrived at the ranch within a few minutes. Matt turned his Suburban off the main driveway and pulled to a stop at a gate in the wire fencing. "I'll open the gate," he said. "Gen, why don't you slide over and drive through once I get it open, then I'll close it behind you."

"Sure." Gen moved over behind the wheel. Matt unlatched the gate and swung it wide, then Gen drove through and pulled to a stop on the other side, returning to the middle of the front seat to wait for Matt.

"The herd's usually over that rise," Matt told Tyler when he'd resumed his place behind the wheel. "There's a small grove of trees where they like to gather. It shelters them from the sun in the summertime and gives them a windbreak in winter."

"Cool," Tyler said.

Matt shifted the SUV into four-wheel-drive and they started over the rolling ground. As predicted, the herd, a group of about a dozen woolly animals, was grouped beneath the trees.

"Wow," Tyler exclaimed. "Can we get out?"

Matt shook his head. "Sorry, dude. A couple of them were hand-reared like Tessie's mom, but most of 'em are pretty wild. They can be dangerous, even if they don't mean to be."

The eight-year-old stared out the window. "Okay. Well, they're cool, anyway."

As they watched, one of the animals, a female, Gen noted by its smaller size, broke from the herd and ambled toward the truck.

"Is that Tessie's mom?" Tyler asked.

"Yep, that's her. She's looking for a handout." Matt shifted around to reach behind the seat and came up with a plastic bag. "Good, I thought I had some bread in here."

He pulled several slices of stale white bread from the bag and handed them to Tyler. "Roll down your window halfway. That's it. Now, hold a slice of bread out to her and she'll come take it."

Tyler did as he was told and the bison cow sauntered over. Up close she was huge, the top of her thickly furred head reaching the upper edge of the door. Tyler turned and glanced at Gen and Matt, his eyes wide, then he held the bread out to the bison. The cow mouthed the slice from his hand, snorting warm, moist breath at him. Tyler laughed and wiped his hand on his jeans.

"Coo-ool," he said, drawing the word out to several syllables. He fed her another slice, and this time he was rewarded with a lick from her long, pink tongue.

Soon the bread was gone and the cow, sensing an end to their charity, wandered back to the herd and dropped her massive head to graze beneath the trees.

Matt started the engine. "Well, see enough?"

"I guess," Tyler said. "That was really neat, though. I wish my dad had been here."

Gen spoke up. "I'm sure we'll get him out here one of these days."

"Good." The boy turned and watched the bison until they were out of sight behind the knoll.

After a few minutes' silence, he faced the front again and looked up at Gen. "Gen, do you like my dad?"

Gen had to stifle a gasp at the suddenness of the question. She shot a glance at Matt and saw that he was grinning broadly. She fought the urge to elbow him in the ribs and turned back to Tyler. "Why sure. I mean, I don't know him very well, but I think he's okay."

Tyler smiled and Gen had a sudden suspicion that "okay" had a very different meaning for the boy than it did for her.

Chapter Six

The next morning, Josh left for work before Gen arrived to see Sue. He told himself he wouldn't have noticed her absence if Tyler hadn't spent half the evening talking about her. And the bison, of course, but Gen Halvorson figured rather prominently in his son's description of his afternoon.

Ty had ended his narrative with "She thinks you're okay, too, Dad."

Josh had to smile. Talk about damning with faint praise. In Ty's vocabulary, though, being "okay" was a good thing, indeed. He wondered if Gen meant it in that way and decided that she probably didn't.

He should have felt relieved, but the thought nagged at him, and the fact that it did aggravated him further. He should be glad she thought he was only "okay." After all, he wasn't interested in dating. Even if he was, there were probably lots of eligible women in the area besides Gen Halvorson, women who weren't into weird alternative medicine and who'd probably think him more than just "okay."

By the time Matt was ready to carpool to the clinic, Josh was irritable and out of sorts. They rode to Halden in near-silence, Josh staring out the window at the winter-browned countryside.

"So, did everything go all right after I left yesterday afternoon?" Matt asked.

Josh recognized the attempt to draw him out of his shell and added guilt to his already sour mood. He had no business taking this out on Matt. The guy was his boss, after all. He turned to the other man and forced a smile. "Yeah. No problems at all. Like you said, it was a pretty quiet afternoon."

"Good." Matt turned his attention back to the road. "Tyler seemed to enjoy seeing the herd."

"He really did," Josh replied. "He told me all about it at bedtime. Thanks for taking him out."

"My pleasure. He's a nice kid. Having him around is good practice."

Josh nodded. "Yeah, you'll have your own here before too long."

"I just hope I'm as good a dad."

"Thanks," Josh managed to murmur, flinching at the unexpected praise, and at the doubt it raised. He wondered if Tyler was starting to experience the same feelings Josh had when he'd moved as a child? Could that be the reason for the boy's recent surliness?

Josh had never considered his own father anything but a good dad, but would a good dad drag his family all over the countryside rather than provide them with a stable home?

Okay, maybe it wasn't a fair comparison. His father had been in the army, so he'd had little choice about moving. Given the circumstances, taking his family with him was the best option.

But Josh had a choice. He didn't have to spend his career as a transient, dragging Tyler with him from place to place. Maybe he wasn't such a good dad, after all.

They arrived at the clinic before he could consider the situation further, and Josh was grateful for the distraction. The day's schedule didn't look too busy, and he remarked on it.

Matt shrugged. "Enjoy it while it lasts. It's nearly baby season. Any day now we'll be up to our ears in lambs, calves and piglets, with the occasional foal thrown in for good measure." He glanced over the reception desk at the schedule. "Speaking of that, you want to take the farm calls today? There are only two so far."

"Sure thing," Josh said. "It'll be a good opportunity to get to know the area."

"Take the Suburban. It's fully stocked and has a navigation system, so you shouldn't have any trouble finding the clients. Elaine will give you the addresses." He dug a set of keys from his pocket and held them out to Josh.

Josh hesitated before taking them. "Will you be able to get back home if there's an emergency?" With a wife in the latter stages of what might be a complicated pregnancy, Matt didn't need to be stranded in town with no way to return to the ranch.

Matt nodded. "We already worked it out. I'll borrow Elaine's car if I need to get home fast. The Suburban has a radio, too, so I can call you back here, assuming there's time."

Josh nodded. "Good. I'm glad there's a plan in place."

Elaine handed him a printout of the client addresses. "There you go, Dr. McBride. The first one, Jack Swenson, has a lame horse. I couldn't get too much information out of Dan Arnold, the second call, but it sounds like he has a pregnant cow that's doing poorly."

"That's okay, Elaine," Josh said. "I'll find out the details when I get there. Swenson, huh? Is he any relation to Hilma?"

"I don't think so," Matt said. "It's a pretty common

name in these parts. A lot of those Scandinavian names are. Plus, just to make it more confusing, we have both Swenson, spelled s-o-n and Swensen, spelled s-e-n. Apparently one ending is Norwegian and the other's Swedish. I can never keep 'em straight, though." He laughed. "Do you need a run-through on the GPS before you go?"

"No, I've used them before," Josh said, smiling. "Any opportunity to play with a new gadget."

Matt grinned back. "I hear ya. The radio in the truck is set to the clinic frequency, so give a yell if you run into trouble."

"Will do." Josh pocketed the addresses and headed out the door.

GEN CHECKED the messages on her cell phone. Only one, and she was on the way to that patient, Jessie Meyers, next. She looked at her watch. She'd had three appointments already today, with four more to go. The hard winter's lingering aftereffect was certainly keeping her occupied.

She punched in the Meyerses' phone number. The line was busy, and Gen suppressed a rush of adrenaline, hoping it wasn't an emergency. This would be Jessie's third child. Gen had delivered both of her previous babies.

The first delivery had gone well, and the last one had been so quick and easy that it was over almost before it started. Gen took a deep breath to calm her nerves. Chances were good that if Jessie had gone into labor and given birth before Gen arrived, there would be no complications.

She pulled to a stop in front of the Meyerses' house and hurried to the front door. A hugely pregnant Jessie Meyers opened it before Gen could knock, and Gen breathed a sigh of relief. "Are you okay? I'm sorry I didn't get your message earlier."

Jessie nodded and brushed a strand of brown hair out of her face. Nicholas, the older of her two sons, was sobbing in the background. "I'm fine. Sorry I didn't catch you before you got here. Nick fell off the swing set and got a bad bump on the head. I thought I'd better have his pediatrician take a look, so I tried to call you to reschedule."

"No problem," Gen said. "I called back, but the line was busy. I was afraid you might have decided to start having your baby without me and were calling Hank to come home and help."

Jessie laughed. "I'd be better off having it myself before calling Hank. He's not too good around blood and stuff, you know."

Gen definitely knew. Hank Meyers was a good-natured bear of a man who worked in one of the local grain elevators, a dangerous and difficult job. To look at him, one would never expect he might be squeamish about his wife's delivery, but sometimes the big, tough guys were the most sensitive about such things, especially with people they cared about. Hank was one of those, and he had yet to make it through the birth of one of his children without fainting.

"Would you like me to drive you to the doctor's office?" Gen suggested. "I have some time before my next patient."

Jessie brightened. "That would be fabulous. I can barely get behind the wheel with this." She patted her round belly. "We can take my car so I can strap the boys in." She paused with a frown. "As long as you're here, would you take a quick look at Nick's head? I don't think it's serious, but he might have lost consciousness for a second or two. I'm sure it wasn't any more than that."

"Of course." Gen tried to keep her voice casual, but a head injury with loss of consciousness was serious. Jessie should have called 911. "Why don't you get the boys' stuff together and get the little one in the car while I look at Nick?"

"Good idea." Jessie gathered up her two-year-old, Jeffrey, her purse and Jeffrey's diaper bag and hauled them out to the car while Gen knelt beside the older boy.

Four-year-old Nick's sobs had subsided, but tears stained his cheeks and an ugly, purple lump stood out on his forehead, emphasizing the paleness of his face. He sat still while Gen gently probed the area around the swelling and checked his eyes for their response to her penlight. Everything looked normal, but that didn't rule out the chance of a concussion or even a fracture.

Jessie came back inside, her brow furrowed. "How is he?"

"His pupil response is good, but the doctor may want to do X-rays or a CT to rule out concussion." Gen put a hand on the young mother's arm. "Jess, you should have called Emergency. It could have been serious. It still might be."

Jessie picked up her son and brushed a stray tear from his cheek. "Gen, you know how it is out here. In the time it takes them to get out to this part of the county, I could have him at the doctor's already. It's only a few blocks away. Besides, he seems fine except for the lump."

Gen knew Jessie was probably right in this instance. Still, Gen didn't like to think about what might have happened if Nick's injury had been more severe. Although Halden had its own volunteer fire department, the town shared emergency medical services with several neighboring communities. The local doctors' offices were able to take care of minor emergencies, but a major trauma usually resulted in a helicopter airlift to the regional hospital in Minot.

"Okay, well, let's get him over there and have the doctor take a look." Gen helped Jessie secure her son in the car seat next to his brother, then assisted in easing her swollen body into the passenger seat.

They drove the few blocks to the Halden medical building, and once inside, Gen took a chair in the waiting area while Jessie and the boys were ushered immediately to an exam room. Gen sat stiffly, hoping Nick was okay. The fact that Jessie had waited to seek treatment for her son made Gen distinctly uncomfortable. At least together they had managed to get Nick here with a minimum of further delay.

Anxious for a distraction, Gen picked up one of the parenting and family magazines on the table beside her and skimmed it for something to take her mind off Nick.

Interspersed with stories about potty-training, childhood diseases, and choosing preschools were items on pregnancy and childbirth that held at least some professional interest for her. For the most part, though, they had little to offer.

The fact that she'd probably never need a subscription to one of these magazines didn't really bother her, she told herself. It was for the best. Children were so fragile. Like Tommy.

What must her parents have gone through with her brother's death? She'd hardly noticed at the time, so caught up had she been in her own grief and in blaming them for being away so often, working long hours to pay her brother's staggering medical bills. But now she recalled their pale, drawn faces, the dark circles under their eyes that spoke of sleepless nights, the hushed arguments after she'd gone to bed.

Strange, she thought, how she'd forgotten so much about those days. Forgotten or suppressed.

Tommy had been a surprise baby, born to her mature parents who thought their baby-care days were long over. She'd been ten years old and fascinated, helping with his care and feeding, determined to be the model big sister.

At the age of two, Tommy became gravely ill and was diagnosed with a congenital heart defect. Surgeries and hospitalizations followed over the years.

When Tommy was home, Gen, by then a teenager, cared for him after school and on nights when her parents worked, tutoring him when he was too ill to attend classes. Some teens would have resented a brother who required so much attention, but Gen loved Tommy, and he adored her. What he lacked in health, he made up for in spirit and intelligence.

He died at the age of eight from complications following transplant surgery. Gen, eighteen, blamed everyone— her parents for not being available when Tommy and she needed them, Tommy's doctors for not being infallible, and herself. Somehow, she thought, she should have been able to save her brother.

Now, years later, she knew she could have done nothing to save him. But his death had been part of the reason she chose her profession.

As a midwife, she could give babies the best possible start in life. As an herbalist, she could provide an alternative in cases where traditional medicine might not be enough. She couldn't have saved Tommy, but she knew she had made a difference in the lives of her patients.

Jessie Meyers stepped through the door to the waiting room, her two boys in tow. Nicholas wore a cold compress taped to his forehead, and Gen breathed a sigh of relief. She stood up. "He's okay?"

Jessie nodded. "Just a goose egg on the head, thank heaven. Thanks again for driving us over. I'm sorry to inconvenience you like this."

Gen shook her head. "It was no trouble. I'm just glad I could help and that it wasn't serious."

She kept an eye on the boys while Jessie settled her bill with the receptionist, then led the way to the car.

JOSH RUBBED the injection site on the cow's flank. "Okay, Mr. Arnold. She should be feeling more like herself soon. It's a good thing you called when you did."

The lanky farmer ran his hand through his brown hair. "Well, I've seen milk fever before, but usually after calving, so I wasn't sure. Didn't want to take any chances, though." He patted the Jersey's neck. "She's one of my best producers."

"It's more common after calving, but can happen before. The injection should prevent a recurrence, but if she doesn't give birth within a week, give us a call and we'll give her another dose of vitamin D. Once she has the calf, I'd like you to supplement her diet with calcium gel. Do you have any on hand?"

"Sure do," Mr. Arnold said. "I usually dose them for a couple days after calving."

"Good. Just what I was going to recommend." Josh closed his treatment kit. "Keep a close eye on her the next few days, especially once she goes into labor, and give us a call if she has any further problems."

"Thanks, Doc." The farmer led the way out of the barn. "Will you come up to the house for a cup of coffee?"

Josh checked his watch. It was still early and no further farm calls had been scheduled. "Sure. I'd appreciate that."

A cup of coffee would go a long way toward cutting through the chill that had settled on him in the barn.

As he followed Mr. Arnold toward the two-story, wood-frame house, Josh noticed a car turn down the Arnold's driveway. He recognized the small sedan. It was Gen. What was she doing here?

His question was answered when the kitchen door opened to reveal a tall blond woman, reed-thin except for her obvious pregnancy. Mrs. Arnold, he assumed, was one of Gen's patients.

"Welcome, Dr. McBride," she said, taking his hand as her husband introduced them. "Come on in." She turned to Mr. Arnold. "Pour him a cup of coffee, Dan, while I wait for Gen."

The farmer gestured Josh to a seat at the big kitchen table, while his wife stepped out onto the porch. "Cream, sugar?" he asked.

"Black's fine," Josh replied. He accepted a steaming mug, then heard the car door slam outside and Gen's greeting to Mrs. Arnold. The sound of her voice sent an unexpected warmth through him.

"So, Matt's here, huh?" Gen was saying as the farmer's wife opened the door for her.

"No, Dr. McBride is doing farm calls today," the woman replied. "Have you met him, yet? He's filling in for Sue Connolly."

Gen hesitated at the door, then willed herself to step into the warm kitchen, telling herself the flush she felt in her cheeks was due only to the change in temperature.

Josh rose from his seat at the table. "Yes," he said. "Ms. Halvorson and I have met." He smiled and held out a hand.

"He's staying at the Connollys'," Gen said. She took his

hand. It was warm from the coffee cup he'd been holding, and was it her imagination, or was that warmth mirrored in his blue eyes? "Hi, Josh."

"Gen, good to see you."

He sounded sincere. Gen caught the glance and smiles that Dan and Kay Arnold exchanged and pulled her hand from Josh's grasp. Maybe she was just self-conscious, but it suddenly seemed that everyone had matchmaking on their minds. She turned to Kay, determined to be businesslike. "So, how are you feeling? Any more morning sickness?"

"No, that's finally stopped, thank goodness. I'm feeling pretty well." Kay Arnold shot another quick look at her husband and Gen could have sworn she winked at him. "Come on back to the bedroom. I know I'm due for a weight check."

Gen was more than happy to leave the awkwardness of the kitchen—and Dan Arnold's smirk—behind. She glanced at Josh. "Guess I'll see you around."

Josh nodded. "Right."

"He's cute," Kay said once they were out of earshot of the kitchen. "No ring, either. Single?" She laughed. "Must be. What woman in her right mind would let that out of her sight?"

Gen sighed. "Oh, don't you start, too." She took a notebook and pen. "So, have you been taking your vitamins?" she asked, pointedly changing the subject.

Kay regarded her with a quizzical expression, but Gen refused to take the bait and Kay finally let the matter drop.

"SHE'S A NICE GIRL." Dan Arnold was still talking about Gen Halvorson as he walked Josh back to the truck. "Real good with animals, too."

Josh nodded absently. "I've noticed that." He pictured

Gen again with Tessie in the barn, perched on the rail of the bison calf's stall while the animal leaned affectionately into her caress. Animals and children, he thought again.

"The things she can do with animals. If I was a superstitious man, it would seem almost like witchcraft."

Josh looked up. "Really?"

"Oh, yeah. She takes care of wild animals when they're hurt or sick." Dan scratched his head, warming to his subject. "I've never seen anything like it. Animals you wouldn't want to get near for fear of getting bit, they just act like they know she's there to help them."

"She treats them?"

The farmer nodded. "Yeah, and not just wild animals. Some folks take their pets to her. They think she's got some kind of power." He laughed. "Like I said, I'm not a superstitious man, but she's definitely got a talent."

He lowered his voice. "Looked at an animal or two of mine. She was kinda reluctant, but she was out here to see my wife and I asked her to check on them. Darned if they didn't turn right around and get better, and she barely touched them."

Josh mulled this news over in his mind. So, Gen Halvorson was practicing veterinary medicine, too, huh? He glanced back at the house, but she was obviously still busy inside. What was she thinking, that she was some kind of mystical healer?

He should have listened to his first instinct, he realized. He'd been willing to put aside his prejudices based on her work with Sue Connolly, but this was too much. It was so typical of the alternative-medicine types he'd known to try and meddle where they had no business. Clearly Gen was no different.

"Well, thanks again, Doc," Dan said, taking Josh's hand in his callused grip. "Say, she's single, you know." He grinned. "You two could make a pretty good team, if you don't mind my saying so."

Josh slid behind the wheel of the Suburban, ignoring the man's last remark. "Thanks, Mr. Arnold, and give us a call if that cow doesn't improve or if she doesn't have that calf within the week." But he was already planning to have a talk with Matt about just what it was that Gen Halvorson was doing around Halden.

Chapter Seven

"Witchcraft?" Matt laughed. "That's a new one on me."

Josh had mentioned the subject of Gen's animal care and Dan Arnold's remarks over coffee at the vet hospital the next morning. He had hoped to talk to Matt about it as soon as he'd returned to the office the previous day, but a surprisingly busy afternoon had intervened. He'd avoided the matter at dinner, not wanting to broach it in front of Sue and Tyler, and by the time he'd finished helping Ty with his homework, there had been no opportunity.

Actually, he was glad for the chance to mull over the situation. He'd been angry after leaving the Arnold ranch, certain that Gen Halvorson was another charlatan out to give people false hope at best or, at worst, scam them out of their hard-earned money. Now that he'd had time to calm down, he thought that surely there was a rational explanation for what she was doing. The Connollys liked and trusted her, and although it was always possible Gen had hoodwinked them, Josh felt the two veterinarians were decent judges of character.

Matt was still laughing. "I've known Dan for years, and this is the first I've heard about rumors of witchcraft."

"Well, I took that part of it with a grain of salt," Josh admitted. "But is Gen practicing veterinary medicine?"

"Technically?" Matt rubbed his chin. "It's possible."

"But that's illegal…" Josh started.

Matt held up his hand, stopping further comment. "She's licensed to rehabilitate wildlife. So, yes, technically, she does sometimes practice veterinary medicine. Sometimes we help her, if it's a serious case or if surgery is required. She's called us in on a number of patients."

He paused and took a sip of his coffee. "Now, if you're asking whether she treats domestic animals, I don't really know. I wouldn't be surprised if the occasional client brings her their dog or cat. She's referred a number of patients to us, so I suspect it happens from time to time. She knows her boundaries, though. She's not going to cross the line."

"Are you sure?" Josh asked. "If Dan Arnold thinks she has some kind of magic power to treat animals, how do you know she's not trading on that? Conning people who might be gullible enough to believe in her?"

The other vet frowned. "Look, what is this about? I know you don't know Gen very well yet, but surely you don't think her capable of that?"

Josh shrugged. "I don't know what to think. I just know that some people who believe in that kind of alternative stuff aren't to be trusted."

Matt leaned back against the edge of his desk. "Gen's a rational woman. She cares about people and animals, but she's not a flake. She knows her stuff. Being a midwife and herbalist pays the bills, but it doesn't keep her busy all the time." He grinned. "Except right now. I've never seen so many pregnant women around Halden."

Josh nodded. "Yeah, I've noticed that, too."

"Anyway," Matt went on, "she does the wildlife stuff in her spare time. Usually, she finds injured animals or people bring them to her, but sometimes I swear the animals find their way to her themselves. It's almost as if they know where to go for help."

Josh gave a snort. "You're starting to sound like Dan Arnold."

Matt shook his head. "Well, I wouldn't call it witchcraft, or anything supernatural, necessarily, but she definitely has a way with them. They seem to know she's there to help. I can't explain it." He looked at Josh closely. "In any case, though, it's no threat to our livelihood. She's not out to compete with us for patients."

Josh subsided under Matt's measuring gaze. Maybe his colleague was right, and he had misjudged Gen Halvorson. Again. He felt a twinge of guilt. Why was he so eager to find some reason to dislike the woman? He pictured her, pale and petite, her long russet hair shining, and felt an entirely different kind of sensation.

Surprised, he banished the thought from his mind and glanced at Matt, who was watching him with interest. "Well, if you're not concerned. I'm sure it's not important. I was just, well, I've had some experience with those types. They prey on people who are desperate for hope, for a cure or even just a little more time with a loved one. I just wanted to make sure…" Josh let the words trail off. This wasn't the time or place to dump his personal history on Matt.

Fortunately, before Matt could ask any more questions, Elaine appeared at the door with the charts for their first patients of the day and the subject was forgotten.

OVER THE NEXT FEW DAYS, Josh realized he was settling into a routine and was shocked to find he was comfortable doing so. Each morning, he woke to a hearty breakfast, prepared by Hilma, and ate with Ty and the Connollys before seeing his son off to school. At work, he and Matt alternated surgery and farm calls, and he discovered they made a good team.

As a substitute veterinarian, he frequently found the dynamics of his working relationships awkward. Sometimes the philosophy or operation of the practice where he was working didn't mesh with his own ideas about treating animals.

As a temporary employee, he often had to make a concerted effort to keep his opinions to himself and maintain his detachment to avoid stepping on his employers' toes, especially if he wanted to be considered for future assignments.

He had no such problems with the Connollys. In fact, for the first time in years, he felt completely at home on a job. The thought both comforted and disturbed him. He'd be leaving in a few weeks. It wouldn't be wise to get too complacent. Even if he could consider staying, Halden was too small a town to support one more veterinarian.

He was surprised to find he wasn't looking forward to leaving, for Ty's sake as well as his own. Josh hadn't seen his son so calm and happy in a long time. Ty was already making friends in school, enjoying his classes and doing well on his assignments. The rebellious streak seemed to have disappeared. Josh was glad to have his easygoing kid back again. He'd been sure Tyler would settle into the new routine and he'd been right. He'd worried for nothing.

Josh sat at Sue Connolly's desk and updated the chart of the rottweiler he'd just spayed. The morning's appointments had kept both him and Matt busy, then Matt had left for farm calls while Josh remained behind to handle the surgery schedule. The patient load for the afternoon was light, as it usually was on heavy surgery days, with only a few vaccination appointments for the techs.

The phone rang and he picked it up. "Yes, Elaine?"

"I have Gen Halvorson on the line. She's calling for Matt, but I told her he's out, so she said she'd talk to you."

Josh started, wondering if Gen was trying to reach Matt because of a change in Sue's condition. No, he thought, she would have called Matt on his cell if that were the case. "Okay, put her on," he told the receptionist.

"One second," Elaine said.

Josh heard the beep of the phone's transfer button, then the distinctive silence of an open phone line. "Gen, it's Josh McBride. What's up?"

"Josh, hi. I was calling for Matt, but Elaine said he was out on a farm call."

He noted an edge to her voice, as if she was uncomfortable or under a strain. Maybe this *was* about Sue, and Gen had been unable to reach Matt. "Is everything okay? Is it Sue?"

"No, Sue's fine. I checked on her a couple hours ago. It's just…" She hesitated, then plunged ahead. "I have an injured fox, probably hit by a car. I'm afraid it needs more care than I can give. I'd bring it in, but I don't want to stress it out further. Matt or Sue usually help with my wild animal patients, but if Matt's tied up, I can stabilize the fox till he gets back."

"No, Gen, I can help. I'll come over. Give me directions to your house."

As he scribbled her instructions on a sheet of paper, Josh

thought over what Matt had told him. Well, now he'd have a chance to see for himself. He wondered if he was making a huge mistake. Somehow he suspected he was.

GEN DOUBLE-CHECKED the heating pad she'd placed under the injured fox, knowing she should have waited for Matt. Now Josh McBride was on his way to her home.

She shivered at the thought, then told herself abruptly to stop being foolish. This was business and she wasn't going to let herself get distracted just because some friends of hers thought she and Josh McBride might have couple potential. She knew better.

The fox lay curled on the heating pad in a small portable cage, watching her with golden eyes, seemingly more curious than fearful. It was here by choice, after all, having dragged itself onto her front step, battered and bleeding with one rear leg tucked close to its haunches.

Gen wondered at that, but this wasn't the first wounded animal that had found its way to her home, not by a long shot. She thought about the instinct or perhaps divine intervention that brought such animals to her, but didn't question it. They came to her for help and she had the ability to aid them. As if they knew that, they allowed her to touch and treat them and seemed resigned to accept whatever fate dealt them at her hands.

Gen had treated the fox for shock, muzzling it gently for her protection, then starting an IV with warmed fluids. The small animal hadn't flinched when she inserted the tiny needle in its front leg vein. Few animals did and she always marveled at that, but it seemed that restraint was more objectionable to them than the actual procedure.

She stabilized and taped the IV in place, then removed

the muzzle. The fox just watched her, his alertness reassuring Gen that his condition might not be too grave.

Out front a car door slammed. *Josh*. Gen closed the cage and went to meet him.

"Thanks for coming," she said, opening the door for him.

"No problem. Matt was just getting back as I left, so I brought the Suburban." He nodded over his shoulder at the SUV. "It has a portable X-ray unit and everything else I might need."

"Good. He's back here." She led the way through the living room.

Josh looked around, trying not to make it appear that he was taking stock of the place. The house was a spacious prairie-square style with a broad porch across the front. It was a lot of house for a single woman, and he wondered if it had been in the family for a long time. It occurred to him that he knew very little about Gen Halvorson.

The living room was neatly and comfortably furnished in soft greens and creamy shades that immediately brought to mind an oasis of calm. Shelves filled with books lined the walls. A plump, longhaired tiger cat eyed him from the seat of an overstuffed chair, while a black-and-white tabby, perched on the front windowsill washed one white foot and studiously ignored him.

Josh followed Gen past a compact dining room and through a bright and tidy kitchen to what had probably been a breakfast room and pantry, but was now a hospital ward and treatment area. Bandages, alcohol and other traditional medical supplies lined neat shelves. He wasn't sure what he expected, but no eye of newt was in evidence and there wasn't a crystal to be seen.

A bank of cages, empty except for a curious rabbit with

a bandaged shoulder, filled one wall. A treatment table with drawers and cabinets stood against another, and in the far corner of the room was a large wire pen in which—Josh found himself doing a double take—a white pelican floated in a kiddie pool. The big bird squawked at him once, as if in greeting.

Gen glanced over her shoulder at Josh. "Ignore him, he's begging for a handout and it's not his feeding time yet." She led the way into the smaller, adjoining room. "The fox is in here."

A pair of larger cages, an incubator, warming lamps and storage cabinets lined the walls of this room. The fox occupied a small carrier on a table in the center. Josh noted the heating pad under the animal and was surprised to see that Gen had also started an IV drip.

Had she done that on her own, he wondered? She was probably trained to do intravenous injections as a midwife, but there was a lot of difference between performing them on a willing human patient and a wild animal. Perhaps the fox had been more subdued when she brought it in. Right now, though, it looked bright eyed and interested in their arrival.

"He looks pretty perky," Josh said. "When did you start the IV?"

"Not long before you got here." Gen glanced at her watch. "I guess it's been about a half hour."

"Where did you find him?"

"Actually he found me. He was on my doorstep when I got back from my morning appointments. He's alert enough that I'm hoping he's not too severely injured internally, but I started fluids to prevent shock, just in case."

Josh thought over what Matt had said about animals

finding their way to Gen. He'd been skeptical, but clearly the other vet hadn't exaggerated. "And he let you insert the IV catheter?"

Gen was close enough that he could smell the light floral perfume she wore. He forced himself to focus on the patient.

She nodded. "I used a light muzzle, but he took it very well." She turned to him. "Shall I get him out?"

"Please," Josh said, adding, "be careful," as she opened the cage.

She looked up at him, her eyes the color of summer grass. "Of course." She reached into the cage and gathered the animal toward her, lifting it cautiously to avoid the injured rear leg, then held the fox cradled to her breast. "Set the cage on the floor and I'll put him on the table."

Josh did as she instructed, noting how the ponytail holding back her thick hair had fallen forward over her shoulder. The red strands mingled with the ruddy fur of the injured fox, making her seem one with the animal, as if she were some kind of nature spirit bound to and communing with one of her creatures.

Gen tilted her head slightly, her expression questioning, and Josh realized he was staring. He blinked and looked away. The spell broken, he waited as she set the animal on the table. She held the fox lightly, her hand under its chin and fingers curved up toward its cheek so she could restrict any aggressive movement, if necessary.

"Are you sure you've got him?" he asked. Though small, the animal could inflict a painful bite if threatened, and rabies was always a concern with any unfamiliar wild animal.

"He's fine," she said. "And I've had my shots," she added with a smile, as if reading his mind.

That only contributed to the otherworldliness of the setting. Here he was, in a strange and beautiful woman's home, handling a wounded creature that should be, by all rights, terrified and defensive. But the fox didn't flinch as Josh raised its lip to check the color of its gums, then palpated it gently, searching for other injuries. The animal behaved almost as if hypnotized by the woman who held it, exhibiting neither fear nor pain.

Of course, Josh thought, he hadn't gotten to the most severe injury. He met Gen's eyes. "Okay, I'm going to examine that leg. He might not appreciate this."

She nodded and he saw that her control of the animal tightened almost imperceptibly. She seemed deep in concentration. Maybe she *was* communing with the fox.

He handled the injured leg. The hip joint was in place, fortunately. "No dislocation," he told Gen, then felt down the leg, noting his findings aloud to her. "Femur's intact, but there's a fracture farther down, feels like it's the tibia. Pulses above and below the fracture are strong. Toes are warm."

He paused and looked at her. "I think he was lucky. If it was a car, it must have been a glancing blow. The leg seems to be the only major injury, and I'll have to X-ray to be sure, but I think it'll heal well without surgery."

Gen released a breath. "That's wonderful news, thank you."

"Let me run out to the truck for the X-ray machine. I'll be back in a minute." He left the house, grateful for a moment away to collect his thoughts. Outside, the day seemed normal with filtered spring sunshine warming an otherwise brisk afternoon, but he couldn't shake the feeling he was participating in something extraordinary.

Josh removed the portable X-ray unit from the Suburban and flicked the On switch of the film processor, a machine about the size of a large computer printer, secured in the bed of the truck. The processor needed several minutes to warm up. By the time he returned with the exposed films, it would probably be ready to go.

He wheeled the unit, a pivoting X-ray head and generator attached to a cart, to the front porch and eased it up the stairs, then returned to the truck for the lead-lined cassette box and aprons.

The box and aprons were heavy by themselves, in addition to the seventy-plus pounds of the X-ray system. It took two trips to get all the equipment to the infirmary. When he returned to the room the second time, he saw that Gen had eased the fox onto its side with the injured leg down, the position he'd need for the exposure. He found himself nodding approval. She knew what she was doing.

Gen watched as he set up the machine. "This is the first time I've had X rays done on an animal here. How are you going to develop the film?"

"The Connollys just had a portable processor installed in the truck. They rigged a blackout curtain to pull around it to make a mobile darkroom, so I can unload the film into the processor without overexposing it." He handed her an apron. "Put this on. It'll probably take both of us to do this and I don't think either of us wants any unnecessary radiation."

He measured the leg and set the controls on the X-ray unit. "How long have you been doing this?" he asked, feeling the need for small talk to distract himself from the effects of her proximity. "Wildlife rehab, I mean."

"I started about five years ago, just after I came back to Halden when my grandmother passed away." Gen stroked the fox's head as she held the animal still for the first exposure. "I inherited the house from her. She had always had animals around—pets, strays, wildlife, everything. I decided the extra room would make a great infirmary, kind of in dedication to her."

"So you haven't always lived here?"

She shook her head. "I was raised here, but left to go to school and lived in Minneapolis for a few years after that."

"Seems like a nice little town." Josh motioned for her to shift the fox for another view.

"It is." She smiled. "I love it here. It really feels like I've come home. I wouldn't want to live anywhere else."

Strangely, Josh could understand that feeling. Something about Halden touched a chord in him, too. It was a sensation he didn't want to examine too closely.

A few minutes later, he was back in the truck, waiting as the processor developed the three films he'd taken of the fox's broken leg. He was impressed with how the animal had lain still, with only the slightest restraint from Gen, as he extended its leg across the film cassette.

When the processor ejected the final film, he checked the pictures on the light box in the truck and smiled at the results. The fracture wasn't minor, but it should be easy to reduce and splint. The fox was lucky, indeed. Josh picked up his medical bag, then, after a moment's thought, gathered up the films, knowing Gen would be interested in seeing them.

She was still holding the fox on the table, gently stroking its cheek and humming softly. The animal appeared utterly relaxed, its eyes half-closed.

"Here we go," Josh said. He held the films, one at a time, up to the ceiling light to show her her break. "It's about what I expected. We'll need to sedate him and reduce the fracture. After that, a splint should immobilize it nicely." He glanced at her and grinned. "He's young, so he'll heal fast, assuming you can keep him from chewing the splint off."

"I don't think that'll be a problem." Gen smiled back.

Somehow, Josh didn't think it would be, either. Together they set and splinted the injured leg, then Gen carried the groggy fox to one of the larger cages and settled him inside. When she returned to the table where Josh was gathering up his equipment, she placed a hand on his.

Josh started. Her hand was hot against his skin, almost feverish, and the contact sent a rush of heat surging through him.

"Thank you, Josh." She looked up at him. "I can't tell you how much I appreciate your help today."

He met her green eyes and knew beyond a doubt that there was something magical about Gen Halvorson after all.

Chapter Eight

Gen watched as Josh drove away from the house, wondering at his sudden departure and whether she'd done something to scare him off. She told herself she didn't care, but she was beginning to suspect that Josh's feelings toward her meant more to her than she wanted to admit.

It wasn't a comfortable sensation, but she could no longer tell herself she wasn't attracted to the handsome veterinarian. She'd touched his hand in friendship and gratitude, but the brief contact had sent her pulse racing. He'd been startled, too, she realized, but she'd thought it was only because of the warmth of her hand, a phenomenon that had always occurred when she worked with animals or people.

She didn't quite know how to explain the condition, but research she'd done indicated that it was a kind of energy flow. She'd learned to focus the energy, channeling it into her patients. The effect was always beneficial, as though she was directing waves of healing into the subject, and she'd grown to consider it a gift. Now it occurred spontaneously, both with her human patients and whenever she handled an animal that needed either medical care or calming.

It usually dissipated when she broke contact with her patients, so she was surprised that Josh had noticed the effect. The more she considered it, though, the more it made sense. Josh was in need of healing. Of that she was certain. Perhaps her gift was responding, without her direction, to that unspoken need. Whatever the case, it had clearly been too much for Josh to handle.

Gen walked back into the infirmary to check on the fox. The animal had begun to stir in the cage, bobbing its head and staring around with wide, unfocused eyes from the sedation that was now wearing off. He'd made no effort as yet to chew the splint, but she'd have to keep watch to insure that he didn't start worrying at it once he was fully awake.

A squawk in the other room shook her from her thoughts, and she turned toward the noise. Simba and Scotty added plaintive meows to second the vote for dinnertime.

"Okay, I'm coming," she called to the hungry animals. She went to feed them, trying to banish thoughts of Josh McBride, but wondering if she'd ever again have a chance to connect with him like she had.

"So, GEN NEEDED help with a fox, huh?" Matt asked when Josh returned to the vet hospital. "How did it go?"

"Fine," Josh replied. He'd spent the drive back to town deep in thought. Full of questions, he nonetheless was reluctant to discuss the situation with Matt.

"Just fine?"

Josh shrugged, sensing that Matt wouldn't have been disappointed if Josh announced that he'd spent the afternoon making passionate love to Gen. The image sent a jolt of arousal through him, followed just as quickly by a wave of anger. The guy had no business playing matchmaker.

Josh was here to do a job, not make a love connection. He'd be leaving Halden soon enough; he didn't need a romantic involvement.

He suppressed the outburst he wanted to make, though, knowing he was reading too much into Matt's simple question. The last thing he needed to do was get defensive. That would really give Matt ammunition.

He decided he had to keep things businesslike, despite the questions he suddenly had about Gen Halvorson.

He shrugged again. "It was a clean break and there were no other serious injuries. That was one lucky fox. I set the leg and splinted it. Should heal pretty quickly."

Matt nodded, clearly disappointed that no more titillating details were forthcoming. "So what did you think of Gen's place?"

Obviously, the other vet wasn't going to let the subject drop. "It's a nice house," Josh said. "She has a pretty decent infirmary set up, too."

"Yeah, she does." Matt paused, then continued. "So, do you feel a little more comfortable about her treating animals?"

Josh felt anything but comfortable where Gen was concerned, and not just with respect to animals. He realized that now. But he replied, "Yeah, as long as she's not practicing medicine on pets. She's not a vet, but she seems to know what she's doing. And you're right, she's not crossing that line."

More than that, he thought, she'd had an almost mystical connection with the animal, but he wasn't going to be the one to broach that subject.

He watched Matt, waiting, hoping the other vet might jump in to enlighten him about what he'd experienced at

Gen's. In addition to his confused feelings about the woman herself, he had to know what kind of phenomenon he'd witnessed. He couldn't bring himself to ask, though.

"Oh, she definitely knows what she's doing," Matt said. "She really has a way with animals, too. It's, um, it's pretty weird. Did you notice?"

Josh let out a breath and nodded. It hadn't been his imagination, then.

And when she'd touched his hand?

He could still feel a lingering trace of the heat from her skin, as though her touch had left an imprint. Somehow, too, he felt, in that moment's touch, she'd been in contact with some deeper part of him, as though all his secrets, his past, were laid bare to her.

The idea frightened him. No one had touched him that deeply, not for years. Not since Kathy.

So he had run. He'd checked his watch, pleaded a busy schedule, and took off like the devil himself was after him.

Josh glanced at Matt and realized the other vet was waiting for a reply. "What do you think it is?"

Matt shook his head. "I don't know. I mean, I think people who become vets usually do so because they have a rapport with animals, but what Gen has is a step beyond that. It's a bond and something more, a healing gift, really. I don't know what to call it, but I wish I had it."

"But what do you think it is, technically?" Josh persisted. He had to know. If Matt gave him a hard time, so what? "She touched me and her hand was hot, almost burning. What is that about?"

"I have no idea, really," Matt said. "Alternative forms of treatment are getting a lot of play these days—reiki, healing-touch therapies, stuff like that. They're supposed to use energy to treat injuries or illnesses. I haven't studied them closely, myself, but there must be something to them because some of them are being accepted into mainstream medicine. I've even heard of cardiology centers and other specialties that use them. I assume what Gen does is along those lines."

Josh shook his head. There might be something to it, but it didn't make him comfortable. If all it took to cure disease was concentrating and focusing energy, then why didn't everyone do it? And why didn't it work in all cases? It was the same with the forms of alternative medicine he'd experienced. Their proponents often touted them as cure-alls, but if they were supposed to magically cure everything, why hadn't they worked for Kathy?

He ran his fingers over the back of the hand Gen had touched, still feeling the sensation of warmth there, wondering if he'd smell her perfume on his skin.

"It all seems a little bit out there, I know," Matt continued. "It wasn't too long ago that acupuncture was considered bizarre, though, and now it's generally accepted, even in veterinary medicine. I've worked with veterinary acupuncturists and I can attest that their treatments do help. Even herbalism isn't that far out. Lots of modern drugs are based on old herbal treatments."

"That's true," Josh admitted. "But it doesn't mean I'm going to start treating patients with decoctions of birch bark or sticking needles in livestock." He hesitated a moment. "At least not those kinds of needles. But I guess you're right. Veterinary acupuncture and herbal medicine have been around for ages."

He had to admit it made sense, regardless of his prejudices. Maybe there was a real, physical explanation for

Gen's "gift," but science simply hadn't yet found the reason. The admission didn't set him at ease, but it did make his experience seem a little less—how had Matt put it—out there?

Josh was suddenly ashamed of himself for running out on Gen. He wondered how she'd feel if she knew the real reason he'd left so abruptly, that he was terrified by the response her touch had ignited.

If he had his way, she'd never know.

The afternoon's appointments barely gave Josh time to think about Gen Halvorson, a situation for which he was truly grateful. An emergency call near closing time kept him at the clinic late, and he drove back to Lilac Hills exhausted, looking forward to seeing Tyler and spending a quiet, well, relatively quiet, evening with his son.

He turned down the long driveway to the ranch and a pleasant sense of homecoming struck him. He really was beginning to think of Lilac Hills as home, he realized, unable to recall the last time he'd felt this way about a place.

As much as he wanted to bask in the feeling, it disturbed him. He couldn't stay at Lilac Hills. There was no way he could make a living in Halden, and it was unlikely that the other small towns in the area could support a vet of their own. Even if that was an option, the Connollys' practice served a large area and he wouldn't want to take clients away from them.

He stopped that train of thought, surprised at himself. He knew that it wouldn't work, so why did his mind continually return to the idea of making a home in Halden?

Before he could examine the thought further, Josh pulled the car to a stop outside the house. As he got out, the front door opened, and Tyler ran down the steps and slammed into him at full speed.

Josh laughed, exaggerating the impact and letting the momentum carry him back against the side of the car. "Whoa! Hey, there, buddy, you're a bundle of energy. You must have had a good day."

"Yeah, it was great," Tyler said, looking up at him. "Mrs. Osborne gave me an A on my history report, and I aced the spelling test. Plus, Bobby McLean and Steve Sumpter are going out for Little League this spring and they asked me if I can join, too. Can I, Dad? Registration is starting next week. It would be really cool to play with the guys."

Josh paused, digesting this new information. Ty had never had the opportunity to play on a team before. The experience would be good for him. Would they be around long enough for him to complete the season, though? Josh didn't know, and he didn't have the heart to tell Ty it might not be a possibility. "We'll see," he said.

Tyler beamed. "Cool." He ran ahead of his father into the house.

Hilma had held dinner, expecting him late, so he, Tyler, and the Connollys gathered around the kitchen table laden with roast beef, potatoes, carrots and fresh green beans. The savory aromas filled the air, mingling with the yeasty scent of Hilma's fresh-baked rolls. Tyler ate as if he hadn't seen food in a week and kept up a running conversation about school, baseball, and the bison calf, Tessie, who he had taken to feeding every afternoon with Hilma's help.

Josh sat quietly, concentrating on his own thoughts. He looked up once to catch Sue Connolly watching him, a tiny frown puckering the smooth skin between her dark eyebrows. Sue's false labor hadn't recurred, but she was still maintaining only light activity around the house as she waited for her due date. Josh wondered what she was thinking. Her expression made him nervous and, for some reason, brought Gen to mind. Gen and Sue were close friends, after all, as well as midwife and patient. He wondered what Gen would tell Sue about his visit to her house today, then felt annoyed at his curiosity.

He looked over at Ty, mentally changing the subject. "Got any homework tonight, son?"

Ty nodded, quickly chewing a bite of potato and swallowing it. "Yeah. Sue's gonna help me, though."

"Oh," Josh said, taken aback.

"If you don't mind," Sue chimed in. "It's one of the few things I can do around here while I'm waiting for this little fella to make an appearance." She patted her tummy. "I've gotta tell you, hanging around the house with nothing to do is boring me to tears. Plus, I'm going to be helping with homework myself in a few years, so I should get in some practice."

Josh shrugged, trying to hide his surprise. "No problem. I'm happy to share the homework load. Especially if it's math." He smiled, hoping it didn't look as forced as it felt.

Ty had never turned to someone else for help with his homework before. Pain cut deep inside Josh, as though some small, private part of him had broken open.

He and Tyler had always been a team, the two of them against the world as they made their way from town to town. Ty's asking for help from Sue was more evidence of his attachment to Halden and to the Connollys.

Knowing it was a good thing for Ty, a sign of his growth and stability, did nothing to ease Josh's hurt. And the bonds his son was creating would make leaving that much harder when the time came.

Josh wondered when Sue would give birth. He hoped it wouldn't be long, because the sooner he and Ty left Halden, the better off they'd both be.

THE NEXT MORNING, Gen arrived to check on Sue before Josh left for work. She'd told herself to wait and avoid him, especially after his alarming departure the day before, but her schedule was light, and rearranging the day to miss Josh seemed rather childish.

Besides, she argued with herself, maybe she'd get a chance to see Tyler. Her visits lately had always occurred while he was at school, and she regretted not seeing him. Maybe if she arrived early enough, she'd catch him before he left.

Ty answered the door when she knocked. "Hi, Gen!" he said, grinning. "Come on in. Everybody's in the kitchen, except Matt. He had an early farm call."

"Thanks, Ty." Gen stepped inside, noting how Tyler seemed completely at home at Lilac Hills, as if he'd made the ranch his own. The observation cheered her. Tyler hadn't seemed outwardly sad or lonely to her before, but she had sensed his need for stability. He'd clearly found that here. She wondered if Josh was aware of the change in his son and what he thought about it.

The idea that Josh might not be cognizant of his son's attitude and how he'd settled into life at the ranch caused her a pang of guilt. Surely he knew what was going on with the boy.

"How have you been?" she asked Tyler.

"Great," he replied, leading the way into the kitchen. "I

might get to sign up for Little League. My dad said 'we'll see,' but that usually means yes."

"That sounds fun. Have you played baseball before?"

"Yeah, but not on a team. We'd get uniforms and everything." He stopped in the kitchen doorway to announce "Gen's here," then took his seat at the table.

"Gen, sit here." Hilma rose and pulled out a chair. "I'll get you some coffee. Have you had breakfast? I have fresh waffles."

"Yes, I've eaten, thanks. Coffee sounds great, though." She gave the older woman a quick hug of greeting, then did the same with Sue before sitting down. "Good morning, Josh. Thanks again for yesterday."

"Morning, Gen." Josh smiled. "You're welcome. How's the fox doing?"

"Good. He came out of the sedative just fine, and he's bright and alert this morning."

"Hasn't chewed the splint off, yet, huh?"

Gen shook her head. "So far, so good. I have an Elizabethan collar to put on him if he starts bothering it."

Tyler laughed. "Wow, that would look pretty funny on a fox."

"I haven't seen too many animals that don't look funny in an Elizabethan collar," Josh said. "They always manage to look embarrassed, too."

Sue nodded. "We sometimes use homemade collars for animals that are too small for the prefab kind. We make them out of old X-ray film sheets and adhesive tape. Talk about looking embarrassed." She chuckled. "And they say animals aren't self-aware."

Gen glanced at Josh and found him watching her. She looked away quickly, feeling her cheeks flush and fighting the annoyance that she knew would only make her blush redder.

Sue was watching her, too, with a pleased and aggravatingly smug expression. She wondered if Josh had noticed her glowing cheeks, but she avoided glancing his way to find out, afraid it would make things worse.

Honestly, she felt like a silly teenager, and Sue's attitude wasn't helping. She could only be grateful that Tyler was too young, and too busy filling each divot in his waffle with maple syrup, to be aware of the undercurrents in the room.

When she finally sneaked a glance at Josh, he was checking his watch. "Eat up, Ty," he said. "It's almost time for your bus."

Gen took the opportunity to shoot a threatening look at Sue who seemed ready to burst out laughing. Hilma's eyes were twinkling merrily, as well. Gen rolled her own eyes. As soon as Josh left, she was going to let both of them have it.

Tyler carried his plate to the sink. "I'm done," he said. "Thanks for breakfast, Hilma. The waffles were awesome. Okay, I'm ready, Dad."

"Got your backpack?" Josh asked. "How about your homework?"

"Yeah, Dad, I've got everything." Tyler's exasperated reply was almost adolescent-perfect. He pulled on his coat, then hugged his father. Josh kissed his son's cheek.

"See you tonight," Josh said. "Have a good day at school."

"Have a good day at work," Ty replied, in the formula that was apparently part of the McBrides' morning routine.

The boy slung his backpack onto one shoulder, started

out of the kitchen, then stopped. He turned and trotted over to her, flinging his free arm around her shoulders for a quick squeeze. "Bye, Gen."

"Bye, Tyler," Gen said, surprised, but able to give him a brief hug in response.

As soon as she released him, the boy darted out the door, leaving Gen fighting the sting of threatening tears.

Chapter Nine

"He's a sweet kid," Sue said. "I think you've become a mother figure."

Gen rolled her eyes, thankful for the distraction afforded by her friend's joke. "Great. That's all I need."

Tyler's attachment to her touched her, though. After all, it was probably the closest she'd get to actually being a mother. She was surprised to find that she liked the feeling. She wasn't so sure how Josh would react to it. Fortunately, he'd departed shortly after Tyler, so she was saved the embarrassment of his hearing Sue's remark.

He'd looked a little stunned when Tyler hugged her. That wasn't the response she'd expected. She wasn't sure what response she'd expected. Josh was a hard man to predict. If his son's affection toward her made him angry, he didn't show it, but it was clear that it bothered him.

As for the hug, Gen was moved beyond words that Tyler thought so much of her. As Sue said, he was a sweet boy.

Gen felt tears well again and blinked them back hard, aware Sue was watching her. She stood up, businesslike. "Well, shall we get you weighed and checked out?"

"Plenty of time for that later," Sue said, not moving

from her seat. "What was up with Josh's visit to your place yesterday?"

"Nothing was up. I assume Matt told you what happened?"

Sue nodded. "He told me about the fox. You can tell me about the hunk."

Gen sighed. "There's nothing to tell. Really. We splinted the broken leg and he left."

"No lingering gazes? No hands brushing one another unintentionally and sending electric tingles through your bodies?"

"What have you been reading lately, girl?" Gen forced a laugh, but her reaction to touching Josh's hand came sharply to mind.

"I'm just a hopeful romantic," Sue replied. "And I'm hopeful that Josh McBride likes you. His son certainly does."

"I think Tyler just misses having a woman in his life. He's fond of you, too," Gen pointed out. "On the other hand, I haven't seen any indication that Josh likes me."

"The object of their affection is usually the last to know. I've seen how he looks at you."

Gen laughed. "Give me a break. When he's not scowling, he looks at me like I have three heads."

"Was he doing either yesterday?"

"Yes, actually, a little. Yesterday was different, though. We were working together."

Sue wiggled her eyebrows. "Maybe you should arrange to work together more often."

"How on earth would I do that?" Gen asked. "Conjure up sick animals out of thin air to get him to make house calls? It's not gonna happen."

"But you admit you're interested?"

"I admit he's attractive. And he seems like a great vet. And I think he tries to be a good dad."

"You have been paying attention." Sue grinned. "Matt says Josh is an excellent vet, and I think he's a good dad, too. Now he just needs to find the right woman to settle down with and give that boy a stable home."

"I'm sure there's someone out there for him," Gen said. "I just don't know if he's ready to settle down."

"Out there, my foot! I know someone right here for him," Sue said. "And one of these days, you're both going to see that. Everyone else does."

Gen just shook her head. "So, are you still thinking about whether to return to work once the baby comes?"

Sue accepted the change of subject with good grace. "Still considering it. Still haven't decided. I love my work, but it's funny, with Tyler around, I keep thinking about what I'd miss by being away from my child every day."

Gen nodded. "I can understand that." What would it be like to see your child grow and learn and change a little every day? She'd probably never experience it for herself, but like Sue, she could see it happening with Tyler, and she resolved to treasure the moments while they lasted.

WHEN MATT HAD PREDICTED that business would pick up soon, he wasn't just trying to sound optimistic, Josh thought. Calls had started coming into the hospital before the office even opened that morning, and the next several days were already packed with appointments and farm calls. Baby season, it seemed, had begun in earnest.

Veterinary intervention wasn't necessary for most animal births. Animals tended to do what came naturally without much human assistance.

Complications were rare on a percentage basis, but with so many animals giving birth in the spring, the total number of appointments nearly doubled. In addition to problem birthings, the vets also had to deal with vaccines, castrations and other seasonal herd maintenance procedures that some farmers or ranchers preferred not to do themselves.

Spring breeding was more common with dogs and cats, too, so puppy and kitten calls rose dramatically, as well.

On normal days, Josh and Matt took turns alternating farm calls and office appointments. One vet would stay at the hospital while the other was in the field, then they'd switch off the following day. During baby season, though, Josh and Matt handled calls at the larger ranches together.

"Sue and I tried taking turns on these big calls," Matt explained as they drove toward a large ranch several miles outside of town. "But we really found it best to have two docs on the scene. The ranchers are usually happy to help out, especially if you need elbow grease more than finesse, but these calls can be overwhelming for one vet. It cuts down the number of clients we can take on a single day, but visits usually aren't emergencies, so we can be a little more flexible about when we fit them in."

"Well, with radio access to the clinic," Josh said, "It's not like you're out of touch if an emergency comes in while you're both in the field." Communications advances had done wonders for modern veterinary practice, he thought. Even critical tests like electrocardiograms could be performed by telephone.

Matt nodded. "Exactly. The techs can stabilize a patient and start treatment while we're on the way back."

They turned down a gravel road. Josh could see a windbreak stand of trees in the distance, a sure sign on the North Dakota prairie that they were approaching a farm or ranch. Trees didn't seem to grow at random out here like they did in the northwest. Generally, if there was more than one tree in a given area, the grove had been planted intentionally.

Josh had thought he'd miss the green canopy of firs and deciduous trees that made his Seattle base of operations a cool and shady place, but he found that he liked the wide-open spaces and the broad, rolling plains. The openness made him feel that he would always know what was coming at him. There would be no surprises when you could see in every direction for miles on end.

Paranoid thought, he mused, wondering what had brought it on. No one was out to get him. So why, lately, was he feeling the urge to run?

As they drew closer to the trees, Josh could make out the details of a house and outbuildings, including a large, red barn. An older man wearing jeans, a short-sleeved plaid shirt, and a ball cap with a tractor-company logo walked forward to meet them as they pulled into the driveway.

Matt climbed out and took the man's offered hand. "Elmer, it's good to see you." He turned toward Josh. "Meet Josh McBride. Dr. McBride is filling in while Sue's on leave. Josh, this is Elmer Swensen. That's s-e-n."

"Would that be the Swedish variety of Swensen?" Josh ventured.

"That's right," the older man said. He took Josh's hand, shaking it briskly. "Good to know you, Doc. I got a couple new calves for you to look over, and about a dozen lambs that need vaccines and tail docking." He looked at

Matt and chewed his lower lip. "You gonna use that new method we talked about with the pressure injector?"

"I thought I'd give it a try," Matt said.

"Good. I know it's gotta be done, but I always hate putting 'em through it." Elmer adjusted the bill of his cap against the morning sunshine. "Come on and check out the calves first, then we can get busy with the lambs."

He led the way to the barn, Matt and Josh following behind. Josh leaned toward Matt. "So what's this method you're going to use for docking lambs?"

"The usual one, basically. Elastrator ring around the tail distal to the caudal fold. I leave a medium to long tail section, long enough to wag. Reduces the risk of prolapse. The difference is that I use a high-pressure injector with local anesthetic to numb the tail under the ring once it's put on. Takes a few seconds longer, but causes less discomfort for the lamb." He glanced at the older man, smiling fondly. "And the owner. Elmer takes good care of his animals. He always wants to do whatever's necessary to keep them comfortable."

"I see," Josh said. "Good." He hadn't met a lot of softhearted ranchers, but he appreciated them when he did. Tail docking wasn't a pleasant procedure, but it was necessary for the health and hygiene of the sheep. Still, it was one of those husbandry techniques that always left him cringing slightly on the animal's behalf. He was completely in favor of any effective method that was easier on the lamb.

Elmer Swensen's barn boasted a recent coat of paint and was brighter and tidier than most of the barns Josh had encountered on farm calls. A hayloft occupied the upper level of the barn, but the ceiling of the main floor was high and hung with modern, fluorescent lighting. Two large bays, one on either side of the double front doors, held bags of feed, dietary supplements, buckets and cleaning supplies, and a variety of other tools and implements.

Beyond the bays, spacious stalls lined each wall. Some of the stalls, meant for horses, had heavy sliding doors with barred windows. Several others were equipped with chest-high rail fencing across the front and broad gates. Two of these stalls were occupied by plump Holstein cows, each with a tiny, black-and-white calf.

"This looks like livestock heaven," Josh couldn't help remarking. Fresh straw filled each scrupulously clean stall and a tall feed rack was brimming with rich timothy hay. A bin of grain and a water trough completed each stall's furnishings.

Elmer nodded. "They have a hard enough life without being uncomfortable in the bargain. It's my duty to provide for them."

Josh glanced at Matt. Swensen's philosophy was unusual. Most farmers or ranchers took care of their animals because good animal husbandry made sense from a business perspective. They weren't extravagant and they didn't treat their stock like pets. Their animals were kept in reasonable comfort, fed decent food, treated medically as long as it was economically realistic to do so and disposed of humanely if it wasn't.

A rare few neglected their animals to the point of cruelty. But hardly any lavished this much consideration on animals meant to serve them.

Matt gave him a wink. "I wish all ranchers took as good care of their animals," he said. "It would make our jobs a lot easier."

Josh nodded. "It sure would." He leaned over the rail to study the first calf.

The animal stood with its gangly legs splayed and its head under its mother's belly, suckling vigorously.

"A little heifer," Josh noted aloud. "She looks good."

Elmer opened the stall gate, and Josh went in while Matt drew syringes of vaccine for him. The Holstein cow turned her head and stared at Josh with thoughtful brown eyes, then, apparently seeing no threat in his presence, stretched her neck toward the hayrack for a mouthful of hay.

Josh pulled the calf from its mother and examined it thoroughly. It was healthy, strong, and less than thrilled at being kept from its nursing, bellowing in Josh's ear as he palpated its abdomen. "Whoa, good set of lungs on her," he said, tugging at the lobe of the assaulted ear.

Matt handed him the syringes, and Josh injected the vaccines. A third vaccine was given orally, the liquid squirted down the calf's throat. The animal seemed to resent that intrusion more than the prick of the needles.

"These are for bacterial and viral dysentery, and salmonella," Josh explained to the rancher, releasing the calf, which loped to her mother's side for protection.

"They'll need more vaccinations," Matt told Elmer, "but you know the routine. Just call the office when they're due and Elaine will set up a farm call."

Josh left the first stall and entered the second. The next Holstein seemed no more concerned with his presence than the first. Her calf was curled up asleep in the corner of the stall, a black-and-white ball nestled in the golden straw. Josh lifted the calf, which cried out once in protest, then stood still as he examined it. Also a heifer, the animal was strong and healthy.

Matt handed him the drawn vaccines and Josh administered them, then freed the calf. It ambled away a few steps, turned to look at Josh accusingly, then tucked its head under its mother, butting her udder, and began to nurse.

"She looks fine, too, Mr. Swensen." Josh stepped out of the stall. "You've got yourself a pair of nice heifer calves."

The older man looked relieved. "Thanks. I always worry about 'em till their first vet check. Can't help it." He closed the stall gate and led the way out of the barn. "I have all the lambs penned outside with their mamas since the weather's nice today. Come on."

The process of tail docking would make for a busy couple hours, although the procedure itself took only about a minute per lamb, even with the use of the pressure-injected anesthetic. Catching a dozen frisky lambs while trying to avoid falling over a herd of restive ewes was another matter, and always the most challenging part of the process.

Eventually they developed a plan. Josh would chase down and capture a lamb, Elmer Swensen would hold it still, and Matt would apply the elastrator band and inject the anesthetic. Then Elmer would release the lamb and take the next one from Josh.

Josh walked toward the nearest lamb, feeling confident that a direct approach would work best. The fluffy white animal waited until he was about three feet away, then sprang upward, its little legs moving like a dancer's, and darted away. Josh had to laugh, despite his frustration. Gamboling lambs were irresistibly cute, his favorite farm babies.

He tried again, this time attempting to fake out the lamb, moving as though to pass by nonchalantly, only to grab it at the last moment. For a member of a species notorious for its lack of intelligence, the lamb seemed to know what he was up to. Again it waited until the last second then, gathering its tiny hooves beneath it, bounced into the air and bounded away. This time it didn't seem quite as cute.

Josh sighed. He was going to have to take a different tack. He ran toward the larger mass of sheep. The animals turned and flowed as one foamy white mass into the corner of the pen. Spreading his arms in an effort to convince them they were enclosed and discourage their flocking back past him along the fence line, he dove for the nearest lamb.

He caught it by one rear leg, but slipped on the muddy ground, falling to his knees. No longer believing themselves trapped, the sheep drifted around and over him, into the center of the pen.

When they were clear of him, Josh lay on his back, muddy and breathless, but still holding the bawling lamb. He looked over his shoulder to see Elmer Swensen laughing and slapping his thigh.

Matt shook his head, grinning. "Good job. At this rate we'll be done with this herd sometime next week, but the entertainment value is worth it. I just wish I'd thought to bring my video camera."

Josh restrained himself from making a rude gesture and rose with the squirming lamb to stagger over to Elmer. Still laughing, the older man took the animal and held it securely while Matt banded its tail. Josh turned back toward the sheep, which were now eyeing him with suspicion.

He had the process down, now, he was sure. He herded the flock into another corner, then waited to grab a lamb as it went by. This time he maintained his balance and carried the wiggling animal back to the treatment area to the applause of both Elmer and Matt.

Before long they were done. Elmer released the last

lamb back into the fold and offered a hand to Josh. "Good job, Doc. You got the hang of that pretty quick."

Josh, sweaty, smelling of lanolin, and covered with mud and sheep dung, wiped his hand on his pants before taking the rancher's. "Thanks. All I can say is that's a bunch of pretty smart sheep you've got there."

"Yep, they tend to know what's what." Elmer grinned, looking over the flock, then paused, narrowing his eyes. "I hate to say this, Doc, but I think you missed one."

Matt and Josh followed his focus. Sure enough, one lamb huddled in the center of flock, no black rubber band on its tail. Matt glanced at Josh and took pity. "I'll get him," he said. "You get the injector ready."

Josh nodded and reached for the medical bag as Matt waded into the mass of sheep. Woolly white bodies flowed around him as he lunged for the remaining lamb. He missed and followed the flock to the other side of the pen. Elmer stepped in to help direct the flock back toward Matt.

"Elmer, you're going to have to get you a couple sheep dogs." The vet reached for the lamb again, but it danced away from his outstretched hand.

"I've thought about it," the older man said. "Guess the flock's big enough now to make it worthwhile."

Matt reached out again, this time grabbing the lamb by the tail. He swung his free hand down under its belly to lift it out of the herd. As he straightened, his foot hit a muddy patch and slipped out from under him.

Josh watched as Matt lost his balance, tipping backward. "Matt, look out," he called. He dropped the elastrator and darted forward.

Before Josh could reach him, the other vet fell while the flock rolled around him like an ocean tide, one large ewe stopping directly behind him. As Matt arched backward over it, the animal jerked and leaped upward, kicking its rear feet like a bucking bronco. Matt's back twisted and his head came down hard against the fence rail. Josh watched as the sheep flowed away from Matt, leaving him lying alone in the mud, unconscious.

Chapter Ten

Josh rose as Sue and Gen entered the waiting room of the hospital at Minot. He stepped forward and took Sue's hands in his. Gen stood behind her friend, her fair skin paler than usual, making the sprinkling of freckles across her nose stand out in sharp contrast.

"How is he?" Sue asked. "What happened?"

Josh guided her to a chair. "He's doing okay. They have him in X-ray now. He fell and hit his head."

Sue bit her lip, tears welling in her eyes.

"It's okay." Josh put an arm around her shoulders, surprised that it felt so natural to do so. He really was beginning to feel like one of the family, and he was glad that in this instance, at least, he could offer comfort like a family member. "The doctor came out before you got here. He says it looks like there are no major injuries. Matt should be on his feet in no time."

"When can I see him?" Sue wiped her hand across her eyes.

"The doctor or nurse should be back shortly. They'll take you to him, then."

He looked over Sue's shoulder at Gen and momentarily found himself lost in the depths of her green eyes.

He had the sense that she was trying to read him, testing him to determine whether he was telling the truth or just providing reassurance for Sue's sake. She seemed to find her answer and nodded.

Josh smiled at her, whatever lay between them at rest for now in this moment of crisis.

"Can I get you anything?" he asked Sue.

Before she could reply, however, a doctor approached them. "Mrs. Connolly?"

Sue stood up. "I'm Sue Connolly. How is my husband?"

The doctor took her hand, and Josh was relieved to recognize that it was in greeting and not to comfort her.

"He's doing fine. No broken bones, just some bruising and a back sprain, plus a bump on the head. You can see him, now. Come with me."

Sue glanced back at Gen, who nodded. "Go ahead. We'll stay out here and let you have some privacy."

"Okay," Sue murmured. "Thanks." Then she followed the doctor down the hall.

Gen sank onto a seat, letting out a relieved whoosh of breath. She looked up at Josh and shook her head. "Thank goodness. She was so worried. We both were. But I was afraid she might go into labor before we could get here."

Josh nodded. "Yeah, that occurred to me, too." He took a seat next to Gen. "I was actually more worried about her than I was about Matt."

"I imagine so." Gen turned to him. "How did it happen?"

Josh told her about the tail docking.

She shook her head again, this time in disbelief. "I wish it hadn't happened so soon after his last injury. I wonder if he'll be out of work for a while?"

"I guess we'll know soon," Josh said. He hadn't considered that possibility, but it was a very real one, especially considering Matt's previous injury.

Josh knew he should be looking forward to the end of this assignment, but for some reason, he'd been avoiding the subject. He hadn't even checked his messages to find out if he had any other potential jobs lined up. That wasn't like him at all. He was usually eager to move on. With Matt laid up, he might be asked to stay in Halden longer than planned. Strangely, the idea didn't bother him.

He glanced at Gen. What would staying in Halden mean to him? And, more importantly, what effect would it have on Tyler?

"It'll really be hard on you if Matt's off work for a while, won't it?" Once more, Gen seemed to know the direction of his thoughts. "I mean, as busy as the practice is this time of year, having only one doctor at the clinic is going to be rough."

Her comments startled him. He hadn't even considered the effect Matt's injury could have on him in the short term. She was right. The hospital was far too busy right now for one vet to handle the load.

The thought occurred to him, but only briefly, that this wasn't the deal he'd signed on for. That he could justifiably break his contract and leave Halden now.

The notion was gone almost as quickly as it had arrived. Despite his intentions in the beginning, Josh now considered Matt and Sue Connolly his friends. He wouldn't leave them in the lurch, even if the job exceeded the limit of his contractual obligations.

As for staying longer than expected, well, he'd cross that bridge later, if it became necessary. For the moment, he didn't know how long Matt might be laid up, so no sense worrying about it till the time came.

He looked up to find Gen watching him and shrugged off a pang of guilt at even considering abandoning the Connollys. Gen seemed as capable of reading him as if his thoughts were etched across his face. He hoped that particular thought wasn't there for her to see. What would she think of him if it were?

The realization that he cared about her opinion was something new to him. He wasn't sure he liked the sensation, but by now there was no way he could fight it. He did care what Gen Halvorson thought, he admitted. More than that, he had a nagging feeling that he was beginning to care about Gen, herself.

"I'm really glad you were out there with Matt, today," she said.

Josh shrugged. "I didn't do much. Matt was pretty lucky. He didn't fall far. The sheep broke the worst of it, although that was probably rougher on his back. The fence post he hit was pretty soggy from the snow, so it wasn't as hard as it might have been."

"And it doesn't hurt that Matt has a hard head." Gen winked at him. "Just ask Sue."

Josh laughed, despite himself, warmth filling him at the awareness that she was comfortable enough to joke with him, especially under these circumstances. Of course, gallows humor was a trait common to those in the medical field, a coping mechanism to carry them through a crisis. Whatever issues he'd had with her, Josh had to admit that he now considered her a colleague of sorts.

The recognition pleased him.

"Did I hear my name being taken in vain?" Matt said over Gen's shoulder.

Josh glanced up to see the Connollys coming toward

them. They looked a sight; Sue with the ungainly waddle of late pregnancy, and Matt in a wheelchair pushed by a nurse, his head swathed in bandages. They stopped at the seating area.

"Who has a hard head?" Matt stared pointedly at Gen, who chuckled.

"You do," Sue said. "The doctor even said so, and now we have X rays to prove it." She sank down next to Gen, breathing hard.

"So, how are you?" Gen looked at Matt, her expression concerned.

Josh noted that, despite his cheerful demeanor, Matt had the look of a man in pain, pale and with a drawn expression around the eyes. And perhaps a bit medicated.

"I'm sore," he admitted. "Didn't hurt anything major, though." He glanced at Josh, his expression sheepish. "I'm going to have to be off my feet for a little while, Josh. I hate to do this to you, especially this time of year. I know this isn't what you signed on for, so I'll understand completely if you have other obligations."

Josh waved his words aside. "Don't even think about it. I'll do whatever I can. We'll work something out." He glanced at Sue and smiled.

The bald relief on Sue's face cut him to the core. "Thanks so much, Josh. We owe you. Really."

"No problem. I'm just glad I can help out." He rose and offered a hand to help her up. "Now we should probably get you both home." He glanced at Matt and grinned. "Before Matt's pain meds kick in and we have to carry him out of here."

IT COULD HAVE BEEN worse, Josh thought, a few days later, as he hurried back from a farm call for the afternoon's appointments. Matt was going to be off work for another week, depending on how he felt, but Josh was handling the workload without too much difficulty.

Many of the farm calls couldn't be avoided since they were either emergencies or seasonal procedures that had to be done within a specific time frame, but most clients understood about the need to reschedule elective surgeries and non-emergency appointments. The Connollys had a loyal clientele who genuinely liked them, and most were happy to do whatever was necessary to accommodate their vets' situation. As a result, Josh and the rest of the staff were keeping their heads above water.

When they brought Matt home from the hospital, Sue volunteered to return to work to see office patients, an offer Gen and Matt had vetoed in no uncertain terms. Josh was relieved. He couldn't imagine how he'd react if she hurt herself or the baby. Not to mention what he'd do if she went into labor.

Josh reached the hospital and entered through the back door. "How's the afternoon looking?" he asked Beth.

"Busy, of course, Doc." The blond technician handed him a thick file folder. "Stan Marshall is in exam two. His Brittany is limping on a front leg."

"Thanks." Josh took the folder and skimmed the details while pulling on his lab coat. Fortunately, after his last call, a difficult calving, the rancher had offered Josh the use of his shower once they'd finished. Otherwise, his office clients might have had to stand upwind while he treated their animals.

He walked into the exam room. Stan Marshall, a stocky, freckled, blond man about Josh's age, stood up. The red-and-white Brittany spaniel sitting on the floor by his feet started to rise as well, but Marshall signaled him to stay as he stepped forward to greet Josh.

"Good to see you, Doc." He shook Josh's hand. "I know you're swamped with the Connollys out, but thanks for taking a look at Buster."

Josh smiled. "No problem. Let's get him up on the table and see what's going on."

Marshall signaled the dog to his side, then lifted him onto the steel exam table. "I was working him out in the field yesterday after dinner. He was fine when I put him back in his kennel, but this morning I saw he was limping."

Josh noticed the dog was keeping his weight off his right front foot. He lifted the foot and flexed it. The dog didn't seem to mind. When he ran his fingers along the metacarpals and down to the toes, however, the dog stirred in discomfort.

"Well, that narrows it down," Josh said. "Would you hold his head? I'm going to have to move those toes so I can see what's happening. He probably won't enjoy it."

"Sure, Doc." Marshall wrapped his arm around the Brittany's neck, holding the dog's head against him.

Josh checked each toe, waiting for a reaction from Buster. The dog flinched and whined softly when he handled the middle toes. Josh reached over to the counter for a pair of electric clippers and trimmed the long hairs from between those toes, revealing red, inflamed skin and a small puncture.

"I think we've found the problem." Josh showed Marshall the wound. "I suspect a foxtail has worked its way up there. We'll need to give him a little anesthesia so we can get it out and clean up the puncture. We'll check him over and make sure there aren't any more in his coat, too."

Foxtails, the barbed seeds of weed grasses, were a common hazard to dogs, especially those with densely furred feet or webbed toes. The seeds would catch in the fur, puncture the skin and become embedded, sometimes working their way far from the entry site, causing pain and infection. Foxtails could enter other areas of the body, but the feet were the most common.

"Great," Marshall said. "Thanks, Doc. I'm glad I brought him to you."

The comment gave Josh pause. The Connollys' hospital was the only veterinary practice for miles. Where else would Stan Marshall have taken his dog? Josh wondered. He had to ask. "You wouldn't have taken Buster all the way to Minot, would you?"

"No." Marshall's freckled face turned pink to the roots of his short, pale hair. "No. It's just that, well…" The stocky man was obviously uncomfortable.

"Go on," Josh said, trying not to push too hard. He had a bad feeling about this.

Marshall shrugged. "One of my neighbors has a cat that's not doing well. She didn't want to wait till she could get an appointment, you being so busy and all. She was going to take it to that midwife gal. Says she's got a way with animals and can make them better just by touching them. She said she didn't have anything to lose, and if the cat got better, that would save her a vet bill."

Midwife gal? "Gen Halvorson?" Josh asked, already knowing what the answer would be.

"That's her." Marshall scratched his head. "My neighbor says there are quite a few folks taking animals to her, what with the Connollys both laid up."

"Is that so?" Josh tried to keep his tone light, fighting his rising anger. Just when he'd started to think Gen was all right, here she was practicing medicine without a license after all, and on the clinic's patients.

No, maybe that was unfair to Gen. It was possible she thought she was doing him and the Connollys a favor, helping out with the workload while Matt was sidelined. Whatever the case, though, he couldn't let it go on. "Well, Mr. Marshall, I'm glad you brought Buster in, too. With all due respect to Ms. Halvorson, I don't think just touching him would get a foxtail out of his foot."

Marshall chuckled but still looked nervous. "No, I guess not." He lifted the dog off the table. "So, should I pick him up tomorrow?"

Josh glanced at his watch, then nodded. "It's late enough that I don't think he'll be ready to go home before closing. You can pick him up tomorrow any time after nine in the morning." Josh looped a nylon leash over Buster's head, then opened the door for the dog's owner.

"Sounds good. See you then." Marshall leaned over to pat the dog, then left. Josh led the Brittany back to the treatment area where he handed the animal over to Terry.

"He's got a foxtail in that foot. Go ahead and give him a pre-anesthetic. I'll see how the rest of the afternoon is shaping up, and we'll take care of him after the last appointment." Then he'd make a call on a certain redheaded midwife.

GEN SANK into her comfortable chair, put her feet up and took a deep, calming breath. Simba and Scotty promptly joined her. The cats took their usual places, Simba on her lap and Scotty on her shoulders. She shifted to accommodate them, then reached for her teacup. The cats twitched and stretched toward the chamomile steam rising from the cup.

"Get your own," Gen said, easing the cup away from Simba's reaching paw. "I deserve this after the day I've had."

What a day! Three of her moms had delivered. It was sheer luck that they'd timed out far enough apart to allow her to attend all three. Fortunately none of them were first babies and all were fast labors. Gen thought back over her career. She'd never had three deliveries in one day before. Maybe it was time for Halden to get a second midwife.

Tomorrow would be another busy day. She'd had to re-schedule a number of her appointments because of the de-liveries. She was just lucky her latest series of childbirth classes was over. She wouldn't have had the strength to teach tonight on top of everything else. She'd barely got-ten her animals fed and treated.

Gen sipped her tea and thumbed through the television schedule. Nothing looked interesting, and the idea of a hot bath and an early bedtime was suddenly very appealing. Perfect, in fact. She rose, discommoding the cats, and climbed the stairs to the bathroom.

She turned on the tap and let steamy water rush into the claw-foot tub, then checked over her assortment of scented bubble baths. Lavender, for relaxation, she thought, and poured a double capful of the purple liquid under the roar-ing tap. She paused and dumped in another capful as the soothing fragrance rose around her. There was no such thing as too many bubbles.

The cats had followed her upstairs and were now shar-ing the cushioned top of the laundry hamper, sitting sphinx-like with their front paws tucked under. Egg-catted, she liked to call their position, because they looked like furry Easter eggs with their backs rounded and no feet visible.

Gen undressed, coiled her hair on top of her head and

secured it with a clip, then slipped into the tub. She left the water running, feeling decadent as the bubbles topped her shoulders.

Raising a bubble-coated hand to turn off the tap, she lay back in the tub, letting her breathing calm and deepen as relaxation settled through her taut muscles. Sinking farther into the water, she felt the bubbles tickle her chin. She closed her eyes and surrendered to the peace and quiet.

The doorbell rang.

Gen shot upright in the tub. Startled, both cats launched themselves off the hamper, upsetting it noisily and racing out of the bathroom in a scrabble of claws and flying fur.

The bell rang again.

Honestly. This was just great.

She supposed she'd have to go see who it was. More of her patients were nearing their due dates. Although she wouldn't normally expect them to show up at her door, she didn't want to risk missing one of them by ignoring her visitor.

"I'm coming," she called, and reluctantly climbed out of the tub, put on her heavy white terry robe and cinched it around her waist.

Her caller was knocking urgently as she made her way down the stairs. "Just a moment," she said, exasperated, and pulled open the door.

Josh McBride stood on her doorstep, and he didn't look happy.

Chapter Eleven

Josh could only stare, his anger momentarily forgotten. Gen stood before him, wrapped in a fluffy white robe. It didn't take much of an intuitive leap for him to realize she wore nothing underneath it.

Her titian hair was piled on her head, but stray tendrils, still damp from her bath or shower, hung loose about her shoulders and clung to the moist, pale skin of her neck, copper against cream. Her green eyes were wide with alarm.

"Josh, what is it? Is it Sue? Or Matt?"

Sue? Josh shook his head. Gen must think he was here on behalf of the Connollys. "No," he said. "I'm not here about Sue or Matt."

"Oh." She waited, one eyebrow raised as if expecting him to explain. When he didn't, she said, "Well, come in. It's cold out." She moved back to let him pass.

He stepped inside reluctantly. This wasn't how he'd pictured their confrontation. On the drive out to her place, he'd mentally rehearsed exactly what he planned to say to her, to tell her in no uncertain terms that she had no business treating animals, especially his patients, no matter how good her intentions. Now, though, everything he'd intended to say was gone.

"So, what can I do for you?" Gen asked.

Josh grasped for something to say, stunned that his mind had gone so completely blank at the sight of her.

"I'm here about the animals." He glanced down at her, noting the swell of her breast where the robe closed, and looked away fast, his face growing warm. "I, uh, I should have called first. Sorry."

Damn, he thought. Why was he apologizing? She was the one in the wrong. This wasn't going the way he'd planned at all.

Gen brightened, her confusion gone. "Oh, of course." She reached for his arm. "I'm glad you're here. I wanted to show you how the fox is doing." She glanced down at herself. "Um, give me a minute to throw on some clothes. I just got out of the tub."

She turned and trotted up the stairs, returning a couple moments later wearing jeans and a T-shirt, her wet hair pulled back into a ponytail.

Still too shell-shocked to react, Josh let her lead him to her infirmary. The pelican continued to occupy the pen in the corner of the room, paddling contentedly in its blue plastic pool. He paused to watch the bird. It tilted its head and stared at him.

"He's nearly healed," Gen said, over her shoulder. "I've been exercising that wing, and he'll be able to fly soon. I hope to release him when he's strong enough. He should rejoin his flock once they come back this spring." She waved Josh to the bank of cages against the wall. "Here's our little foxy fella. He hasn't chewed off the splint, but he has managed to get the bandage wet, so we should probably change it."

Gen opened the cage door and reached inside. Josh held

his breath, not knowing what kind of reaction to expect from the animal. Its behavior had been docile when they'd initially treated it, but that could have been due to shock from its injuries. A healthy animal might not react as calmly, and Gen wasn't even wearing gloves to protect her from a bite.

He needn't have worried. Gen had apparently won the wild creature's trust during her time as its caretaker. That, or there really was something to this power of hers.

The fox allowed her to pick it up and carry it to the treatment table where she placed it on a towel to keep the splint from banging against the hard surface. The animal was bright, alert, and a little plump under his russet coat.

"Looks like he's eating well," Josh remarked, his earlier irritation losing out to professional curiosity.

"He's an eating machine," Gen said, laughing. "And if he doesn't get some exercise, he'll be big as Simba before long. I just hope he'll be able to return to the wild. I try not to domesticate them, but sometimes they get so used to regular feeding, it's hard to make the break."

Josh nodded, examining the splinted leg while she restrained the fox and struggling to keep his mind on what he was doing. Gen was close enough that she radiated warmth from her bath and the fragrance of lavender surrounded her. It was a change from her customary lilac scent, but he liked it just as much.

He caught his breath, forcing his attention back to the animal he was treating. "Okay, he doesn't seem uncomfortable when I move the leg. Let's take off the splint and have a look, then rewrap it. If you want to move him into a bigger cage, it'll give him a chance to walk around and regain some strength above the break."

"Good idea. I have a large kennel in the other room that should work nicely. I'll get scissors for the bandages. Keep a hand on him for just a second."

She left the table and came back a moment later with a pair of blunt-ended bandage scissors, then took control of the fox once more, holding its leg out so Josh could cut away the wrappings that held the splint in place.

He peeled back the strips of adhesive tape that sealed the bandage, then unwound the stretchy pink wrapping material that secured the spoonlike plastic splint to the fox's leg. The wrap stuck to itself without adhesive, making bandaging and, more importantly, bandage removal, a lot less trouble, especially on a furry animal.

Josh set the splint and damp bandages aside and examined the leg. It seemed small and pale compared to the uninjured limbs, but that was mostly the effect of having the hair mashed down and moistened by the wrapping. He flexed the leg gently. The fox seemed unconcerned.

"It's looking good," Josh said. "He doesn't appear to have any discomfort in the joints above and below the fracture. Let's go ahead and wrap him back up with the splint. I think another couple weeks should do it, but you'll want to change the bandages again if he gets them wet or soiled."

"Wonderful," Gen said. "I can't thank you enough for your help."

"No problem." The reason for his visit came back to Josh all at once, although strangely, it didn't seem as important as it had when he'd arrived. At first he wasn't sure how to introduce the subject, then decided the direct approach was best. "Uh, listen, Gen," he said, "there's actually another reason I came by."

"Oh?" She looked up from the fox, emerald eyes meeting his. "What's that?"

He took a deep breath, hesitating, not wanting to sound accusing. The realization annoyed him. Talk about thinking with parts other than his brain. He had a valid point to make, but just the sight, and scent, of a beautiful, barely dressed woman had been enough to make him throw all his intentions out the window.

His anger, at himself this time, flared again, strengthening his resolve. He plunged ahead. "A client mentioned that people were bringing their pets to you because they couldn't get appointments at the hospital with Sue and Matt out of commission."

There, he thought, it was out, and he hadn't been nasty about it. He waited, seeing her weigh her response.

"A couple of your clients have come to me," she admitted. "I told them I can't practice veterinary medicine, but I did look at some of their pets." She went on, rapidly, "Josh, I'm sorry. I know it was wrong, but I couldn't turn them away with sick animals or send them home to wait for an opening at the hospital. The people of this town are like my family. I had to be there for them."

Josh opened his mouth, then closed it again, understanding dawning. He was a heel. How could he have been so stupid?

Of course she couldn't turn away a sick animal. What else could she do but try to offer assistance? It was her way, and her gift. She wasn't trying to steal the Connollys' patients, just to provide help at a difficult time.

"I'd have called you if there was anything serious, Josh." Gen shook her head. "They were just so worried about their pets. For some people, their animals are all they have. They needed me. I couldn't just do nothing."

Josh sighed. "You're right, you couldn't. I guess I didn't really think about your situation."

Between them, the fox shifted, alert and agitated as if mirroring their anxiety. It moved toward the edge of the table, and Josh reached out, a reflexive motion to try to catch it, fearful that it might fall off.

The fox flinched, avoiding Josh's grasp while ducking its head toward his hand. He felt a sharp pinch in the soft tissue below his right thumb.

The animal jumped toward Gen, clearly seeing her as its protector. She restrained the animal while Josh looked down at his palm. A droplet of blood welled from a small puncture.

"Oh, he bit you." Gen's voice was warm with concern. She scooped up the now-compliant fox and placed it in its cage, then turned back to him. "Are you okay?"

Josh examined the wound. "It's nothing. Just a nip. I must have startled him. I thought he was going to fall." He laughed. "Didn't want to risk another broken leg."

"Let me take a look." Before he could protest, she took his hand in both of hers and checked the wound closely. Then she drew him to the sink, releasing him just long enough to turn on the water.

"Looks like only one tooth broke the skin. The others just scratched you a bit." She looked up at him. "I assume you've had your shots?"

He nodded. "Tetanus and rabies, both boostered in the last year."

"Good." Holding his palm under the running stream of warm water, she squeezed the wound gently to encourage bleeding. Josh winced but didn't resist. She was doing exactly what he would have done.

She squirted a dark red-brown liquid onto his hand from a plastic bottle — iodine soap, Josh guessed — and worked it into the area of the wound. Her fingers were hot against his skin as her gift, her power, enveloped him.

He glanced sideways at her, furtively watching. She was intent on washing the wound, but didn't appear to be concentrating or meditating to produce the effect. The phenomenon seemed to just happen without any conscious effort.

She massaged the antiseptic soap deep into the muscles of his palm. The heat of her hands flowed up his arm, becoming pulsing, tingling waves of energy. Suddenly it seemed that every wall of defense he had was being battered down.

Before he could think about what he was doing, he curved his free arm around her slender waist, pulled her against him and bent his head to her mouth.

Her lips were as hot as her hands, as if the healing fire permeated every part of her. He expected her to resist; indeed a part of him hoped she would, hoped she would make it easier for him to release her, to come to his senses and treat this like the mistake he knew it to be.

She didn't. The motion of her hands changed from therapy to caress, then stilled altogether, her lips parting under his.

Josh pulled back slowly, opening his eyes. Hers were still closed, her long lashes sweeping her cheeks. Lord, she was beautiful. And he had no business doing this. No business being here.

He let her go and she looked at him, something like fear in her expression. She knew it was as pointless as he did, he thought. Good. That would make it easier for both of them.

"I'm sorry," he started.

"Are you?" she asked. "Why?"

He shook his head. "It was a mistake. I…" He glanced toward the door. "I have to go."

Gen nodded and stepped back, freeing his injured hand. "That should be clean enough, now." She reached for a paper towel, giving it to him.

He wrapped the towel around his palm and made his escape, leaving her standing alone at the sink, the water still running behind her.

GEN RAN A HAND across her eyes, feeling the beginning throb of a headache. What had she done? How could she have let things go that far?

Even as she thought it, she knew the truth. She had let it happen because she was falling for Josh McBride. She'd wanted him to kiss her. Maybe she'd even wanted more.

Why?

He wasn't ready for a relationship and she didn't need one. He certainly wasn't husband material. He was barely able to make a stable life for himself and his son. Was she that hard up for man in her life?

She shook her head, knowing all her arguments were pointless. Sue had summed it up perfectly. Josh was a good man. A good vet, a good father. Whatever issues he had about intimacy, about commitment, were minor compared to the basic fact that he was a man worthy of love. And in need of love.

Josh wanted her, too. She had no doubts about that. There had been passion in his kiss. Desire, raw and intense. How long had it been, she wondered, since he'd allowed himself to love someone? How long since he'd let down the walls that guarded his heart?

She'd known when they first touched that Josh needed healing. Now she only hoped that she could help him without losing her own heart in the process.

JOSH LAY AWAKE long into the night thinking about what had gone wrong. He should have stayed mad and gotten to the point of his visit from the beginning. Instead, he let her distract him.

How could he have prevented that, though, when she showed up at the door dressed only in a bathrobe?

The image of her, warm and wet and lavender scented, filled his thoughts. More than once tonight he'd imagined himself untying that robe, sliding it from her shoulders.

Would she have stopped him? From the passion in her kiss, he knew she wouldn't have. Neither of them would have stopped until it was too late.

He groaned and rolled onto his side. Oh, yeah, that would have solved a lot, he thought. He'd be in worse shape than he was now.

It's nothing, Josh told himself. His interest, his arousal, was only because it had been such a long time since he was with a woman. Even as he thought it, he knew that he was fooling himself.

Gen wasn't just any woman, or even just a beautiful woman. She had depth and grace, warmth. Yeah, God knows she had warmth. His palm still felt as though it glowed from her touch. He'd never experienced anything like that before.

If he wasn't careful, he was going to be in a world of hurt. Gen was the kind of woman a man fell in love with. That is, if the man in question didn't have a job that would take him away in a few weeks' time.

There could be nothing permanent with Gen Halvorson, and he wasn't willing to hurt her by offering her less than permanence.

The thought amazed him as he realized its implications. He was falling for Gen. As hard as he'd tried not to, as often as he'd attempted to find reasons to dislike her or distrust her, he was falling beyond any hope of saving himself.

Chapter Twelve

Gen folded a blanket around the red-faced infant, swaddling her securely, then placed the tiny bundle into Jessie Meyers's arms. Jessie's own face was nearly as red as the baby's, her brown hair soaked with perspiration, but her dark eyes were sparkling as she held her daughter for the first time.

"We never thought we'd have a girl. Did we, Hank?" This last she directed at her husband, who sat doubled over in a chair at the foot of the bed.

"No," Hank Meyers's voice was muffled but surprisingly strong, coming as it did from between his knees. "We expected another boy. I'm glad it's a girl."

Gen met Jessie's grin and smiled back. This was the third Meyers baby she'd delivered and in every case Hank had yet to make it through without passing out. She'd have expected him to be used to this by now, but apparently one delivery every two years wasn't enough to accustom him to the process.

He took his weakness in stride, though, and didn't seem the least embarrassed by it. For Jessie's sake, he held up as long as he could, and, to his credit, this time he'd made it through most of her brief labor. Then he subsided onto the chair set aside for that purpose, pale and shaky, as his eyes rolled back beneath their lids. Gen had leaped to his side, bending him forward to place his head between his knees and he'd awakened almost immediately.

"How are you doing, Hank?" Gen leaned over him. "Can I get you anything?"

The big man shook his head. "Nope. I'm fine, Gen. Just give me a minute."

Jessie spoke up. "Hurry up, hon. Your daughter is waiting."

Gen glanced down at the back of Hank's head. She really didn't want him to get up before he was ready. Hank was about six foot five and more than twice her weight. If he passed out while upright, he'd fall hard, and there was no way she'd be able to move him.

"Take your time, Hank," she said. "She's not going anywhere." She winked at Jessie, and the new mother sighed, gazing with fond exasperation at her husband.

Before long, Hank rose, still pale but steady on his feet, and went to his wife's side. He stood, seemingly enraptured, staring at the baby in Jessie's arms. He reached out a tentative finger and touched a tiny but perfectly formed hand. Reflexively, the baby curled her little fingers around his.

He looked across at Gen, wonder and love written clearly on his strong features, and she felt tears well in her eyes. No matter how busy she got or how hard she worked, this always made it worthwhile. Now it was time for her to go, though, to let the parents and their new arrival bond.

She checked on Jessie one last time, taking her hand. "Your parents and the boys are waiting. Shall I send them in?"

Jessie nodded and squeezed Gen's hand, her own eyes filled with tears. "Thanks, Gen."

Gen patted her hand. "You're welcome." She gestured

toward the bedside table. "I left your aftercare instructions, but you know the routine. Call me or your doctor if you have any problems or questions."

She turned to Hank and was surprised when the man lifted her off her feet into a bear hug. She patted his back. "You take it easy, and make sure she gets some rest."

He set her down and nodded. "I will. Thanks, Gen."

Gen opened the door of the birthing room and waved in the rest of the family. Jessie's parents had come to watch Nicholas and Jeffrey during the delivery, the Meyers having decided the boys were both a bit too young to witness the birth. Now they'd stay to help out until Jessie got back on her feet. They shepherded in the boys, who were eager to meet their new sister, pausing to shake hands and thank Gen.

Gen closed the door on the babble of happy voices and stood alone in the corridor. She sighed deeply as the familiar postdelivery letdown settled over her, an aftereffect of the adrenaline rush that had carried her since Jessie's early-morning phone call had startled her out of a fitful sleep.

It was a normal reaction, but somehow, it felt different this time. She'd never felt quite so alone after a delivery before.

She knew the cause, too, even if she didn't want to admit it. Her mind flashed back to last night and Josh McBride's kiss.

It didn't seem fair that something so perfect could have been a mistake, but it was. She knew it and so did he. That's why he'd left so abruptly. If he hadn't...

She shook her head, trying to clear away the image of what might have been.

It was good that he'd gone.

She bit her lip, wondering how many times she'd have to tell herself that before she began to believe it.

JOSH TURNED BACK the cocker spaniel's earflap and grimaced at the musty odor and inflamed ear canal. Mrs. Gentry hadn't been doing a very good job of treating her dog's ears.

He pulled a few strands of damp, waxy hair from the ear, and Greta growled. Apparently, her owner had done just enough to make her irritable.

He looked over the dog's head at the small, white-haired lady. "It's pretty nasty in there. I'd like to keep her for a few hours and get these flushed out and treated."

The woman's wizened face crinkled more deeply with her frown. "Oh, do I have to leave her? She really hates to stay here."

Well, she wouldn't have to if you'd just treated her ears, Josh thought, but he didn't say it aloud. "I know she won't enjoy it, but we do need to get them cleaned out. She'll feel a lot better once they're treated."

"Will you have to anesthetize her?"

Josh shook his head. "I don't think so." He looked at the dog and she glared back. Muzzle her, maybe, but anesthesia probably wouldn't be needed. "Would you like us to call you first if we need to?"

"No, no, you do what you have to." Mrs. Gentry scratched the dog's head. Greta glared at her, too. "If she comes home groggy, at least she won't be mad at me all night."

"Great." He pressed the intercom button to contact the front desk, not wanting to release his restraining hold on the dog in her present temper. "Elaine, please send in Terry. I have an ear flush for her and Beth."

Terry came in, carefully lifted the dog to the floor and led her out of the room. Josh watched with Mrs. Gentry, then escorted the elderly lady to the front desk. "Call us around four o'clock. She should be ready to go then, even if we have to sedate her."

Mrs. Gentry nodded. "Thank you, Doctor. Take care of her."

"We will."

She left, and Josh leaned over the desk to see what other appointments were on the schedule. Baby season had hit a lull and for the first time in days, the vet hospital wasn't busy. Josh had thought he'd be grateful for a break, but he was wrong. Today seemed as if it would never end.

"You look like you could use a cup of coffee," Elaine said, eyeing him. "Late night?"

He glanced at the older woman. There was no trace of guile in her expression, and no way she could have known about his visit to Gen the night before. She seemed genuinely concerned about him. He'd be touched if he weren't in such a rotten mood.

"Insomnia," he said. He must have sounded more snappish than usual because Elaine's eyebrows raised toward the gray curls on her forehead.

He relented. "Took a long time to get to sleep, then I was waking up all night long. Must have had too much of Hilma's coffee at dinner."

Elaine nodded. "That'll do it. Hilma's coffee is pretty well-known around here. I think we still have some of Gen Halvorson's nice herbal tea back in the lounge. She blended it just for us. It might be better for you. Shall I bring you a cup?"

Josh shook his head, fighting the urge to snap at her

again. He didn't want coffee or tea, especially Gen's private blend. He wanted…what exactly did he want?

The image of the gorgeous redhead, wrapped in a white terry robe sprang to mind. "No. Thanks. Maybe later."

He wandered to the front window and stared out at the main street of Halden, forcing the picture of Gen from his thoughts.

Gray-white clouds were rolling overhead. The temperature had dropped and there was a distinctly moist feel to the air. Only this morning it had been sunny and mild, not that he'd paid much attention in his state of mind.

"Looks like snow," Elaine said behind him. "The weather report was forecasting a storm."

"Is that common this late in the season? At home, it's usually warmed up pretty well by March." He turned to her. Snow could make his farm calls treacherous, not to mention cold and unpleasant. Just what he needed, he thought.

"That may be the case in Seattle, but not here. Some of our worst blizzards have been in late winter or early spring." Elaine placed files for the afternoon's remaining appointments in a divided holder on the countertop. "It's likely it won't amount to much, though. They always seem to predict the worst, but we usually don't get hit as badly as they expect." She gave him a conspiratorial wink. "I think they just do it to drive up the ratings."

Josh nodded. He could picture the local television stations vying for viewers with sensationalized weather forecasts and titillating farm-commodity reports. Oh well, they did it in Seattle, too. Except for the farm-commodities part. He couldn't recall ever seeing a report on hog futures when he was back home.

Home. It was funny that he thought of Seattle as home

when he was hardly ever there. If the truth were known, he really had few ties to any place. Tyler had even less. His son had always been happy to be wherever Josh was, but Josh was beginning to wonder if Tyler really wanted a place of their own.

Halden spoke to him of home. Halden and Gen Halvorson. He pushed the thoughts away once more. He'd sorted this all through last night, lying awake. It was pointless to go over it again.

Work, that was what he needed. He looked at the clock over the reception desk. A half hour until his next appointment. He wished they were busier. A good rush of patients would take his mind off his troubles. Too bad the Connollys' clients were so accommodating about their absence.

Josh bit back a sigh. He had to do something to keep busy. "I guess I'll go see how the girls are doing with Greta," he told Elaine. "Call me when my next appointment gets here." He'd turned to leave the waiting room when the front door opened and three small bundled figures entered, one of them carrying something wrapped in a towel.

Josh stepped forward. The boy with the bundle was Tyler. "Son, what are you doing here? Why aren't you in school?"

Tyler ran to him. "Dad, Bobby and Steve and me, we found a bird on the playground. We think it's a hawk. It's hurt. Can you help him?"

Josh glanced at the two other boys—Ty's friends from school. They watched him with something like awe, mingled with worry for the bird they'd rescued. Josh nodded. "I'll take a look."

He took the towel-wrapped bird from Ty, then herded the boys through the waiting room and into one of the exam rooms, and laid the hawk on the table.

Blood stained the white towel he recognized as one from Ty's gym bag. He folded back the edges. The bird, a large northern harrier, or marsh hawk, lay trembling, its eyes closed. Josh saw at once the deep laceration in its breast and a probable broken wing. Other internal injuries were also likely.

"You can make him better, can't you, Dad?"

Josh looked into Ty's worried blue eyes, feeling the weight of the other boys' stares on him as well. He heard the front door open and a rush of feet in the waiting room.

The intercom buzzed.

"Emergency, Doctor," Elaine's voice filled the room.

Josh folded the towel back over the bird. "Wait here, boys," he said, and left the room.

Chaos greeted him in the waiting area. Stan Marshall stood in the center of the room cradling a red-and-white spaniel that lay limp in his arms. Blood ran from the dog's nose and shattered head, and from numerous cuts along its body.

"He was chasing a rabbit," Marshall said, his face pale. "He ran out into the road. There was a truck."

Josh nodded and gestured him through the door to the exam rooms. "Bring him on back. This is Buster, right?"

Terry and Beth had come up from treating Greta in response to Elaine's call. They took a quick look, then ran ahead of Josh to prepare emergency supplies.

Josh led Mr. Marshall downstairs to the treatment area and had him lay the dog on the table. Beth clipped a patch of hair from the right front leg, then expertly inserted an IV catheter hooked up to a bag of warm Ringer's solution. She secured the catheter to the leg while Josh examined the dog.

The visible injuries were severe, including a fractured

rear leg, but Josh was more concerned with what he couldn't see. From the animal's labored breathing and the lack of lung and heart sounds, he suspected a ruptured diaphragm, a tear in the membrane that separated the thoracic and abdominal cavities.

He told Marshall his concerns. "We'll need to take an X ray to be sure, but if it's a diaphragmatic hernia, he'll need surgery immediately."

Without surgery, abdominal organs could intrude into the chest cavity, possibly compressing the heart and lungs and causing death.

Stan Marshall nodded. "Do whatever you need to do to save him, Doc. Whatever it takes."

"I'll do my best, Stan." Josh turned to Terry. "Take Mr. Marshall back to the waiting room and get his contact information. Beth, we have to move fast. Let's get him into the X-ray room. I'll lift him and you handle the IV."

Terry led Mr. Marshall out of the treatment area, while Josh carefully lifted the dog and carried him, Beth trailing with the attached IV tubing and fluid bag, to the X-ray table in the next room.

"Dad?"

Josh looked up. Tyler stood in the doorway of the X-ray room. Damn, he'd forgotten about his son and the injured hawk.

He glanced at Beth. "Go ahead and do two thoracic views. I'll be right back." It would take a few minutes for her to take and develop the X rays, enough time for him to deal with the harrier.

Beth nodded and began positioning Buster on the X-ray table, while Josh went to his son. He put his arm around Ty's shoulder and led him back to the exam room.

"Son, we have an emergency and I'm probably going to have to do surgery this afternoon. You and your friends need to get back to school so you can catch your buses home." He looked meaningfully at the other boys.

Ty stared up at him. "But what about the hawk?"

The bird was still hanging on, its breathing slow but steady. The injuries were grave, however, and it was likely it wouldn't survive long.

Josh shook his head. "He's hurt pretty bad, son. I don't think he'll make it and he's probably in a lot of pain."

Tears welled in Tyler's blue eyes and Josh steeled himself for what was to come.

"I think the best thing for him is to put him down."

"But why?" The tears had overflowed now and were running down Ty's cheeks. The other boys looked stricken. "You can save him."

"I don't think I can," Josh said. "And it's not fair to let him suffer when whatever I try is not going to do any good."

"But, Dad…"

Josh fought back a surge of impatience. He didn't have time for this. Buster was a patient he could save, given the chance, but the more time he spent arguing with Tyler, the more the dog's condition would deteriorate.

"Ty, I said no, and that's it." He bundled the harrier in its towel and picked it up, cradling it gently despite his irritation. "Now, I have to get back to my patient. You boys head on back to school."

He walked out of the exam room, leaving the three eight-year-olds in tears behind him.

This is the right decision, he told himself. The bird probably wouldn't survive no matter what he did. So why did he feel so miserable about it?

He carried the harrier to a cage and placed it inside, still bundled in the towel, then went to the controlled drug cabinet for euthanasia solution.

Before he could unlock the cabinet, Beth's voice came over the intercom. "Dr. McBride, I have the films ready, but Buster's crashing."

Josh stuffed the keys back in his pocket. Despite what he'd told the boys, the bird was probably too far gone to actually feel much pain. Euthanizing it could wait until he'd finished treating Buster. He hurried to the X-ray room.

FOUR HOURS LATER, he sutured the last of Buster's lacerations and gave the dog an antibiotic injection.

The Brittany had crashed on the X-ray table due to air in the stomach, which caused that organ to compress the heart. Changing his position had relieved the pressure for the short term, allowing his heart to continue to function.

Josh repaired the ruptured diaphragm, the most critical injury, first. A complex procedure, it required artificial respiration for the dog, because the tear in the diaphragm prevented the lungs from expanding once Josh made the thoracic incision to repair it. Beth operated the anesthesia machine, manually compressing the rebreathing bag to inflate the dog's lungs regularly, keeping his system oxygenated.

Once the herniation was repaired, Josh closed the incision and withdrew air from the thoracic cavity so the lungs could function normally.

Then he turned his attention to the broken leg and other wounds. The femoral fracture required pinning, another involved procedure. Josh took great care to maintain sterility in any surgery, but especially with orthopedic cases.

Bone infections could result in the loss of a limb or even cause life-threatening septicemia.

Once the major injuries were repaired, Josh concentrated on the minor ones, a number of deep lacerations and abrasions. These, ironically, would probably cause Buster more discomfort during recovery than his serious wounds.

His head injuries appeared worse than they probably were, although Josh couldn't completely rule out the possibility of brain trauma. Buster's pupil response had been normal and he'd shown no signs of cerebral involvement thus far, so Josh was keeping his fingers crossed that the worst was behind him.

"Okay, that's it." Josh stepped back from the surgery table and assessed the dog's breathing and gum color. Buster looked pretty good, all things considered. Now, all the dog had to do was make it through recovery. "Put him on a warming blanket and keep the fluids going."

Beth nodded. "Will do." She yawned. "I can stay and monitor him if you want to run home for dinner."

Josh shook his head. "No, that's okay. I have some paperwork to do and, oh…" He remembered the harrier Ty and his friends had brought in. He'd better take care of that, assuming the bird hadn't already died. "Go ahead and take off once you're done," he told Beth and went to the controlled-drug cabinet.

He measured a syringe of the clear, blue-tinted liquid and entered the amount in the hospital's drug log. Then he capped the syringe and went to the ward where he'd left the bird.

The cage door stood open. Blood stained the newsprint that lined the floor of the cage, but the towel and bird were gone.

Chapter Thirteen

Josh's first thought was that the bird had died and one of the technicians had removed it from the cage. On further consideration, though, he realized that both young women had been busy treating Greta, the cocker spaniel, when Ty and his friends brought in the hawk. It was likely that neither of the techs knew it was here.

That left Ty.

Josh shook his head in disbelief. His son and the other boys must have taken the harrier after Buster came in. But where could they have gone?

Only one place made any sense. Ty had taken the bird to Gen.

"Buster's all settled on a warming pad and he's starting to wake up," Beth said behind him. She paused at the counter to stare out the window. "Look, Doc. It's snowing."

Josh looked up. Fat, white flakes whirled past the window, sparkling in the light of the streetlamp. Snow already covered the parking lot; it had clearly been coming down for some time, and the wind was blowing hard.

An icy hand seemed to grip Josh's heart. How long ago had Ty left the clinic? What if he was caught in the snow on the way to Gen's?

Josh turned to Beth. "I have to go. I think my son might be out in the storm. I have to find him."

Beth's face went ashen. "Oh no, Doc. Go. I'll stay with Buster. I wanted to see what the wind was doing before I went home, anyway. I didn't want to get stranded halfway…" She frowned with concern, as though realizing the effect of her words on Josh. "Can I call someone? The sheriff? Matt?"

"Call the sheriff, then call Matt and get me Gen Halvorson's number. You can radio it to me in the Suburban." He pulled on his coat and grabbed the keys to the truck, then dashed out into the storm.

By the time Josh reached the highway outside of Halden, snow was blowing across the road and beginning to drift in the wide ditches on either side of the freeway. Gusts buffeted the Suburban.

Please, God, he prayed, let Tyler have already gotten to Gen's.

He had to be there. The alternative didn't bear considering.

"Doc, come in, over."

Josh flinched as Beth's voice sounded over the radio. He grabbed for the mike. "Beth, it's Josh. Were you able to reach the sheriff and the Connollys? Over."

"No, Doc. The storm's worse than I thought and it looks like phone service is down. I tried the Connollys' cell and no luck there, either. I have Gen's number, but I doubt if you'll be able to reach her. Over."

Josh felt cold sweat break out on his forehead despite the chill weather. "Give it to me just in case." He pulled a pen from his pocket and scribbled the number on a notepad attached to the dashboard. "Sounds like you'd better stay put. Will you be all right at the hospital?"

"Sure," the tech said. "We always lay in emergency provisions in case of blizzards or tornadoes. I'll be fine."

Blizzard. The word settled painfully in the pit of Josh's stomach. He forced a light tone into his voice. "Good. The patients are all treated for tonight and everything's charted in case you're on your own with them tomorrow. If anyone is able to get in touch with you at the hospital, let them know about Ty and that I think he's gone to Gen's. That's where I'm headed. Over."

"Will do. Don't worry about things at this end. And, um, Doc?"

"Yeah?"

"There's emergency survival gear in the truck." She paused, as if hesitant to go on. Then she continued. "If you go off the road, don't try to walk anywhere. Stay with the truck until rescue comes. We lose a couple people every winter when they get stranded and leave their cars to try and walk to shelter in a blizzard. Over."

"Thanks. I'll remember," Josh said. "Over and out."

The radio went quiet and the sounds of the storm closed in around him. He picked up his cell phone and tried Gen's number. Nothing. The lighted display read No Service.

Josh slammed the phone onto the passenger seat and gripped the steering wheel, fighting to hold the Suburban on the road against the icy gusts.

"IT'S BAD, isn't it?" Tyler tore his attention from the injured hawk to look up at Gen.

"Bad enough," Gen said, knowing she had to be honest with the boy. "I think he has a good chance, though." She finished bandaging the injured wing. The laceration in the harrier's chest, now closed with butterfly strips, was deep but not life threatening. She'd treated worse. Now if they could only prevent shock and infection, the raptor might pull through.

Gen watched the snow falling past the window, visible against the dark night in the lights from her porch, her anxiety mounting not over the bird but the storm. Snow had been coming down hard for some time, and the wind was already fierce by the time Tyler had surprised her by showing up on her doorstep, the hawk bundled in his backpack. Gen had invited him in, then tried without success to call both the veterinary hospital and Lilac Hills. Phone service was apparently out.

She glanced at the eight-year-old, who had turned his attention back to the bird and stood stroking its silver-gray head. It was nearly seven o'clock. Josh or the Connollys would have missed Tyler by now. They must be frantic.

Now that the bird was stabilized, she considered loading the boy up in her car and trying to make it to the ranch, but the way the storm looked, she didn't dare. All she needed was to get them stranded in a snowdrift. She couldn't risk Josh's son. At least here he was safe, even if his father didn't know where he was.

She tried both her phone and cell again. Nothing. Forcing a smile, she turned to Tyler. "I think it's past your dinnertime. Are you hungry?"

He nodded, looking suddenly shy. "A little."

Gen lifted the bandaged bird. "Okay, you grab the IV bag and we'll get him settled. Then I'll put dinner on. Do you like grilled-cheese sandwiches?"

"Yeah," Tyler said eagerly, betraying his hunger.

With the boy's help, she carried the bird to a cage. Then

Tyler followed her to the kitchen, where she handed him plates and silverware.

"Go ahead and put those on the table. Would you like milk to drink?" She tried to sound normal. Honesty was one thing, but there was no point in letting Tyler know how worried she was about the storm.

Gen had been through her share of blizzards on the plains, and her grandmother's house had weathered decades of them. She wasn't concerned for Tyler and herself. They'd be fine. She kept picturing Josh, sick with worry once he realized his son was missing.

Would Josh have a clue where Tyler might have gone, she wondered? The boy had been reluctant to talk much about how he'd found the bird or why he'd come to her. If he'd been at Lilac Hills when he discovered the injured creature, surely Matt or Sue could have treated it, even in their present conditions. Instead of taking it to them, he'd loaded up his bicycle and ridden to her house.

A thought began to nag at her. Maybe Tyler had come to her because his father had refused to treat the hawk. If so, she might well find herself in Josh's bad graces once more.

The boy finished setting the table and came over to watch as she heated a griddle and buttered bread for the sandwiches.

"American cheese or cheddar?" Gen asked.

"American, please."

"Want to get a carton of milk from the fridge and put it on the table? I'll get glasses."

"Sure," Tyler said. He opened the refrigerator and pulled out a half gallon of milk, then carried it to the table.

"Ty," Gen asked, "did your dad look at the hawk before you brought it to me?"

He didn't answer right away and Gen turned to face him. She could almost see him struggling for a reply, reluctant to lie to her and yet not eager for her to know the truth.

Finally he replied. "We found the hawk at school and took him to the vet hospital first. Me and Bobby and Steve." Tears formed in Tyler's blue eyes. "My dad said it was in pain and probably would die. He was going to put it to sleep. Then the dog came in and he had to work on him instead, so I took the hawk and brought him to Steve's. Then I borrowed Steve's bike to come here."

Tears ran down his cheeks. "Why would he tell me the hawk was going to die? Why wouldn't he try and save it? You said it would be okay."

"Oh, Ty." Gen held out her arms and Tyler ran to her, wrapping his own small arms around her. "I'm sure your dad was doing what he thought best," she said.

"The hawk looked pretty bad and a lot of birds would have died of those injuries," she went on. "He still might die, but he's young and strong, and I think he's got a good chance to recover. If one of your dad's clients came in with an emergency, though, your dad had to handle that. Especially if he knew he could save the client's pet, and thought that maybe he wouldn't be able to save the hawk, too.

"Sometimes veterinarians and doctors have to make hard decisions, Ty," she continued. "If a patient is so sick or hurt that they can't be saved, sometimes the doctor has to decide to let them die so he can use the time to save another patient."

She looked down at Ty's pale, tear-streaked face. "Do you understand?"

Tyler nodded. "I think so. But how come you were able

to save him?" He frowned, then gazed at her intently. "Some of the kids say you're magic. Are you?"

Gen shook her head, smiling. "No, I'm not magic, Ty. Animals trust me to help them. They let me take care of them and a lot of times they get well. Not always, though, same as with your dad."

"It makes him sad when they don't get well," Ty said.

"It makes me sad, too." Gen ran a hand through the boy's blond hair. "And I'm sure it made him sad when he thought the hawk would die."

Tyler looked up at her, then his brow knit as another thought seemed to occur to him. "Do you think he'll be mad that I came here?"

Gen shrugged. "I don't know," she said honestly. Josh probably wouldn't be happy about it, but she imagined that at this point, he was more worried about his son than angry at him. He'd probably be happy simply to know Tyler was all right.

The boy was quiet as he and Gen ate their supper of grilled-cheese sandwiches, potato chips and dill pickles. Gen wondered if he was thinking of the consequences of his trip to her house.

After eating, Gen cleared the table while Tyler went to check on the bird. As she put the dishes in the sink, she heard a car door slam and looked out the window. She recognized the Connollys' Suburban. It had to be Josh. Well, she thought, they'd find out soon enough if he was angry at Tyler and at her.

She went to the front door, opening it before he knocked.

"Tyler?" he asked, the strain obvious in his voice.

"He's here. I've been trying to call but the phones are down." She stepped back to let him in out of the cold.

"I know. I've been calling your number and the Connollys' since leaving the clinic." He ran a hand through his hair to brush the snowflakes away, leaving it standing damp and disheveled. To Gen he looked like a little boy who'd been playing in the snow. She recalled running her hands through his sandy hair the night before and her breath caught at the memory of his arms around her, his mouth on hers.

"Hi, Dad."

She and Josh turned toward the doorway to the dining room. Ty stood there, looking small and nervous.

"Son, thank God." Josh held out his arms and Tyler ran to him, his hesitancy gone. "I was so worried about you." He hugged the boy tight, then held him at arm's length. "What were you thinking going out in the storm like that?"

Tyler shrugged. "It wasn't snowing hard when I left Steve's. I didn't think it would get bad. I was just afraid the hawk would die if I didn't bring it to Gen." Tears filled his eyes and spilled onto his cheeks. "Don't be mad, Dad. I only wanted to make it better."

Josh shook his head. "I'm not mad. I'm just relieved that you're all right." He looked up at Gen. "And I'm sorry he imposed on you like this."

Gen couldn't believe what she was hearing. He wasn't angry with her. Instead he was apologizing to her. "It was no imposition," she said. "I'm glad I could help, and that Ty made it here safe. I'm glad you got here safely, too. The storm is getting more dangerous by the minute."

Josh bit his lip. "I didn't have much choice. So, how's the hawk?"

"Come see, Dad." Ty grabbed his father's hand. "Gen

fixed him up. She thinks he's going to be okay." He led Josh through the house to the infirmary, with Gen following. "Are you hungry, Dad? Gen made us some great grilled-cheese sandwiches." He looked at her over his shoulder. "Can you make a sandwich for my dad, Gèn?"

Josh stopped. "Ty, I think we've inconvenienced Gen enough for one night."

"Have you eaten?" Gen asked.

"Well, no," Josh admitted. "I came right from the hospital as soon as I realized where Ty might have gone."

Gen waved them toward the infirmary. "Take him to see the hawk, Ty, and I'll put a couple more sandwiches on the griddle." She stayed in the kitchen while Ty and Josh went on ahead.

"Here he is." Ty stopped in front of one of the cages. "He looks good, doesn't he?"

Josh examined the bird through the metal barred door. It did look good, studying him back with alert, piercing eyes. An IV catheter was secured into a vein of the uninjured wing, while the other wing was expertly wrapped. The deep chest laceration had been closed with adhesive suture strips and didn't look nearly as bad as it had when he'd examined the creature earlier. Tyler was right. The harrier was probably going to make it.

"Isn't it great?" Ty said, stretching a finger through the bars to stroke the bird's free wing. "It's like magic, but Gen says she's not really magic. She just has a way with animals, like you do. It's pretty cool, huh?"

Josh nodded. "Yep, it's cool."

"Are you glad he's going to be okay?"

Josh looked at his son. "Of course, I'm glad."

"Because I told Gen you were sad when animals died."

Ty had moved his hand so he could touch the bird's head. The hawk seemed unperturbed by this caress.

"Careful, he might bite," Josh said.

"No he won't, Dad." Ty shook his head. "He knows we're here to help."

Josh stifled a sigh, not sure whether to be grateful for or disturbed by the effects of Gen's benevolent influence. He'd have to make it clear to Ty that one didn't reach out and pet wild animals. That could wait, though. For now, his son was safe and that was all he cared about.

"Sandwiches are ready," Gen called from the kitchen.

Tyler grabbed Josh's hand. "Come on."

He led his father into the other room, pausing at the refrigerator to take out the carton of milk. Clearly Ty felt at home at Gen's, Josh thought, not at all sure how that made him feel. He glanced at Gen. She was smiling fondly at his son.

"Thank you, Ty," she said, and turned to Josh. "Have a seat. I made you two sandwiches, but if that's not enough, I have more bread and cheese, so let me know."

Josh sat down. "Two should be plenty, thanks." Gen set the sandwiches in front of him, along with a glass for the milk, then put the potato chips and pickles on the table. "I really hate to intrude like this," he said.

Gen shook her head. "It's no intrusion at all. Besides, I owe you for taking care of the fox. How is the bite wound, by the way?"

"Fine. It should heal fast." He tried to sound casual, but memories of his previous visit and the kiss they'd shared came flooding back. He pictured Gen in his arms, eyes closed, her long lashes sweeping her cheeks. He caught his breath and showed her his hand.

She took it in hers, turning it over to inspect his palm. The bite was a small red dot. She touched it and he flinched.

"I'm sorry," she said, frowning. "Is it sore?"

"No. I guess I just expected it to be." He smiled, feeling sheepish. How could he explain that he was reacting to the mere touch of her hand?

Simple. He couldn't. He caught and held Gen's eyes as he struggled for something to say.

"May I have some milk, please?" Tyler asked.

Gen released Josh's hand and rose. "Sure. I'll get a glass. I think I have some cookies around here, too." She glanced at Josh. "We didn't have dessert earlier."

"Well, we'd better do that, then." Josh patted his son's head, relieved that the spell had been broken. He watched Gen as she walked to the counter and filled a plate with cookies from a cat-shaped cookie jar.

She looked back at him, as if she could feel his attention, and he slid his eyes away quickly, only to watch her again when she turned back to the counter. He felt like a schoolboy, sneaking glances at her, but he found he couldn't help himself. She was beautiful, and she moved with a dancer's grace. He could have watched her for hours.

"What kind are they?" Ty asked.

"Chocolate chip," Gen replied, starting to set the plate on the table.

"I'm allergic to chocolate," Ty said.

Gen looked taken aback for a second, but before Josh could respond to his son's fib, Tyler said, "Not really," and giggled.

"Stinker," Gen laughed. "Just for that, maybe you shouldn't have any." She raised the cookies.

"Hey!" Ty reached for them, but Gen lifted the plate away from his outstretched hand, then set it quickly on the table and hugged Ty, tickling his ribs.

He laughed loudly and wriggled from her grasp. Watching them, Josh realized how long it had been since his son had laughed that way or roughhoused with someone other than him. Now he was obviously attached to this beautiful woman, an attachment Josh was beginning to share.

"Okay, you two," he said. "Knock it off before something gets broken. Like the cookies."

"Well, we can't have that." Grinning, Gen collapsed onto a chair while Ty grabbed two cookies and darted to the other side of the kitchen lest she try to take them back.

"Did you make these?" Tyler asked. "They're really good."

"Sure did," Gen said. "From scratch, even."

"What's scratch?" Ty munched his second cookie.

"That's when someone makes something from flour and sugar and stuff, instead of from a mix," Josh replied.

"Wow." Ty was clearly impressed. "How come you don't have your own kids?"

Gen seemed to catch her breath, then smiled. "I haven't found the right daddy for my kids, yet."

Josh had the feeling she was trying to avoid his gaze. He turned to Ty. "Eat up. We've bothered Gen long enough. We have to try to get back to the ranch."

A gust of wind shook the old house and the lights flickered. Gen frowned and looked toward the window. Josh followed her glance, then got up and walked to the back door to check outside.

The heavy snow seemed to be falling horizontally as the wind caught it and whipped it past the house. Josh couldn't see beyond the end of the front sidewalk. Beyond that, the porch lights illuminated only a swirl of white.

The lights flickered again, then the house went dark as Tyler gave an exclamation of surprise.

Josh turned to him and Gen. "I think we might have to impose a little longer."

Chapter Fourteen

"Are we going to be snowed in, Dad?" Excitement filled Ty's voice.

"I don't know about snowed in," Gen said. "But I think it's too dangerous for you to go anywhere till the storm subsides."

She made her way to the kitchen counter and felt around in one of the drawers until she found a flashlight. Clicking the switch experimentally, she sighed with relief when the light came on. "Whew! I wasn't sure the batteries were still good."

"Is there anything I can help with?" Josh asked.

Gen shook her head, then realizing he probably couldn't make out her gesture in the darkened kitchen, she said, "No, stay put. I'll track down some light sticks." She moved to the pantry and opened the door, then searched it by flashlight until she found what she was looking for.

"What's a light stick?" Ty asked.

"It's a plastic tube filled with two chemicals that glow when they're mixed together." Gen held up her quarry, shining the light on a handful of individually wrapped sticks. She took one from its package, snapped it and shook the liquid contents together. An eerie blue glow filled the kitchen. "Hmm," she said. "I'd forgotten I had blue ones."

"Cool," Tyler breathed. "Can I see one?"

Gen handed him a stick. "Just unwrap it, then bend it like you're trying to snap it in half. When it pops, shake the tube to mix the chemicals and it'll glow."

Ty snapped the tube and shook it. His produced a whitish light. "Neat."

"Great idea," Josh said. "Safer than candles, too."

"Exactly, especially with kids and animals running around. Not as romantic, though, I suppose." Gen realized what she was saying. Mentioning romance after last night wasn't the best idea. She hurriedly changed the subject. "I have a wood stove, so we should be okay for heat. Water's something else again."

She turned the handle on the faucet. The pipes gurgled with the release of air, but nothing else came out. "The house is on a well and the pump's electric, so it looks like that's out of commission till the power's back on. I have bottled water stocked up, though, so we're fine. No baths, though."

The subject of baths brought last night to mind once more and Gen felt her cheeks flush. What was she doing? she wondered. Tempting fate?

She was thankful for the dim light, hopeful that the McBrides wouldn't be able to see her blush in the glow of the light stick.

Here she was with Josh McBride stranded at her home, Gen thought. What would Sue say if she knew?

In a way, Gen wished Sue did know. The Connollys were bound to be worried about Josh and Tyler, especially since Ty should have arrived home on the bus hours earlier.

"Let me check the phones again," she said. "Sue and Matt are probably frantic." She reached for the wall phone while Josh took out his cell. Her phone was still dead. She glanced at Josh.

He shook his head. "Still no service. I'm hoping they'll assume I'm stuck at the vet hospital and that Ty's with me and not worry." He rose and ran a hand through his hair, looking out the window at the blowing snow. "How long do you think this will last?"

Gen shrugged. "I don't know. Overnight, probably. Maybe longer. The side roads might be impassable for a couple days after the storm ends, unless we get a warm snap to melt the drifts once the blizzard blows through."

"Can that happen?"

"Sure. Weather's pretty changeable here in the spring. After all, yesterday was warm, and today it's like the Arctic. Who knows what tomorrow will bring." She went back to the pantry and pulled out two gallon jugs of bottled water, then used one to fill a teakettle. She forced a light tone into her voice. "I don't know about you, but I think this weather calls for some cocoa. Luckily the stove's gas, so we can at least count on hot food for the duration."

Josh nodded and sat back down at the table. "Cocoa sounds good. Thanks."

"Do you have marshmallows?" Tyler asked.

Gen laughed. "Well, it wouldn't be hot cocoa without marshmallows, would it? I have some games, too. Want to play Monopoly, or Scrabble?"

"Monopoly," Tyler said. "I always beat my dad at that."

"Wait here and keep an eye on the kettle," Gen said. "I'll be right back." She took her flashlight and left the room.

"This is cool," Ty said. "I've never been snowed in before."

Josh ruffled his son's hair. "You're not scared, huh?"

"No. I'm glad we're at Gen's. She's really nice."

"She sure is." Josh knew now that he meant it.

Gen returned a few moments later with the board game and a battery-powered lantern. She set both on the table and switched on the lantern. "This will give us a little more light to play by."

Behind her, on the stove, the teakettle whistled. "Josh, would you set up the board while I get the hot chocolate? Ty, if you want to take the flashlight and look in the pantry, I think there's a bag of marshmallows on the second shelf."

"Sure." Tyler grabbed the light and ran to the pantry, while Josh busied himself taking the Monopoly board from the box and setting up the play money and game pieces.

Gen returned to the table carrying a tray with mugs of steaming cocoa. She set a mug in front of Josh and put one at Tyler's place, then took the third to her own seat as Ty returned with the marshmallows. Immediately, two cats leaped onto the table, the larger of them plopping right on top of the game board, nearly covering it, while the other climbed onto Gen's shoulder.

Gen shook her head. "Oh no you don't." She slid the big cat off the board. "Josh, Tyler, I don't think you've been introduced to Scotty and Simba. This is Scotty." She pointed to the black-and-white cat draped over her shoulder like a fur stole. "I call him the Cling-on cat because he likes to attach himself to me whenever I'm home. The fluffy yellow one is Simba. He's a sweetie, but he doesn't have much going on between the ears, if you get my drift."

Tyler laughed and stroked Simba, who still lay sprawled

on the table in the exact spot to which Gen had moved him. The big cat rolled onto his back, purring, a clear request for a belly rub.

"I don't know," Josh said, eyeing the feline. "He doesn't seem too stupid to me."

"Well, he is fairly bright where food and petting are concerned," Gen admitted. "Let me get them off the table. Not that they're spoiled or anything."

"Oh, I want them to stay," Tyler protested. "Can they?"

Gen looked at Josh. Her green eyes danced in the soft lantern light. "I don't care," he said. "I'm a cat lover. A dog lover, too, of course. I try to give equal time."

"Well," Gen relented. "If we can keep them off the game, I guess it's all right."

Scotty remained perched on Gen's shoulders, apparently content to watch rather than actively participate in the game. Simba rolled upright and stood slowly, his plume of a tail held high, then sauntered across the table and stepped down into Tyler's lap.

A clearly delighted Ty scratched the cat behind the ears, then offered him a marshmallow, which the animal took daintily in his mouth.

Josh laughed. "I guess he knows who the soft touch is around here, too."

With the cats out of the way, the McBrides and Gen played Monopoly by lamplight in the snug kitchen while outside, the wind continued to roar.

Before long, Josh noticed that Tyler was beginning to yawn with increasing frequency. He looked at his watch. It was after ten. "You're looking sleepy, buddy," he said to his son. "I know you probably won't have school tomorrow, but I think it's time for you to hit the sack."

Ty yawned again. "Oh, Dad, can't I stay up? It's a special occasion."

Josh shook his head. "No. You've had a busy afternoon and you need to get a good night's sleep." He turned to Gen. "If you have a spare couch and a blanket, I'll get him settled down."

"You're not sleeping on couches," Gen said. "This is a big house and I have plenty of room. My guest room has a bed and everything." She rose and picked up the lantern, then grabbed the open jug of water from the counter. "Come on, gentlemen. I'll show you to your room."

She was on her way before Josh could protest again that they'd already inconvenienced her enough. He and Ty followed her through the house and up the stairs, Simba and Scotty trailing in their wake. The house felt different in the dark, but no less welcoming despite the danger that roiled outside. To Josh it was an island of peace in the center of chaos, and he felt his anxiety melting away.

At the top of the stairs, Gen turned the corner and entered a spacious guest room that held a queen bed. She set the lantern on the dressing table and turned to Josh and Ty. "The bathroom is right across the hall. I'll put a light stick in there for you and you can use this water for toothbrushing and drinking. I always keep a couple new toothbrushes and toothpaste in the medicine cabinet. Help yourself to those. I'm afraid I don't have any guy's pajamas, though."

Josh shrugged. "That's okay. That's what T-shirts are for. You've provided more than enough already."

Outside, the wind howled around the house and tree branches scraped against the bedroom window.

"Can I keep my light stick in here with me?" Ty asked, a quiver in his voice. He'd carried the glowing plastic tube upstairs with him and now held it clenched in his fist. "I'm too old to be scared of the dark," he assured them. "I just want it in case I have to get up."

Josh smiled. "Sure you can keep it, son. A night-light is a good idea."

Ty normally wasn't afraid of the dark, but here in a strange house with a noisy storm outside, Josh wasn't surprised that his son might be scared, despite his protests to the contrary. He glanced at Gen. She was watching Ty, her expression one of genuine fondness.

"I'll head back downstairs," she said after a moment's silence. "Let me know if you need anything else. Oh, and you'll want to leave the door open when you do go to sleep. Otherwise the heat from the wood stove won't warm the room." She left them the lantern and closed the door on her way out.

The wind howled again.

"Are you going to bed now, too?" Ty asked his father, sounding hopeful.

"Probably not yet," Josh said, but realizing Ty didn't want to be left alone, added, "I'll stay with you till you're asleep, though." He turned back the covers and fluffed up a pillow. "Go brush your teeth, then come on back."

"Okay." Ty went across the hall to the bathroom while Josh stepped to the window and looked out.

In the darkness outside, Josh could see little, only the heavy flakes falling close to the window, showing no sign of slackening. Beyond those, everything became a blur of rushing white against the darkness. They'd made the right decision, he thought. No one with any sense would head out in this kind of weather. They were safe and warm here, and in no danger.

In no danger to life and limb, anyway. The danger to his heart was something else again. It was a hazard he hadn't had to contend with for years, a fact that made the peril all the more profound.

He pictured Gen alone downstairs and a tremor went through him. She was so close and so desirable.

Speaking of sense, he thought with annoyance, if he had any, he'd stay up here with Ty and go to bed. He could climb under the covers and stay put until the cold, safe light of day made things a little clearer. Safer.

Sense was in short supply lately, though, especially where Gen was concerned. The kiss they'd shared had been special to him, but he didn't know what, if anything, it meant to her. She hadn't brought up the subject, but with Tyler around, there had been no opportunity.

It was something they needed to talk about. As much as he'd like to avoid the topic, he resolved to find that opportunity.

Ty returned from the bathroom, pulled off his jeans and crawled under the covers.

Josh walked over to sit by him on the bed. "Warm enough?"

The eight-year-old nodded, his face illuminated by the light stick on his pillow.

"You're going to be sleeping on that before morning if you leave it there," Josh said. "Want to put it on the nightstand?"

"Okay." Ty handed him the tube.

Josh set it on the low table beside the bed, still easily within his son's reach. "There, that's better. Ready to go to sleep?"

Something scratched at the door.

Ty started and sat up. "What's that?"

"I don't know." Josh went to the door, opening it a crack. He laughed. "Looks like we have company."

He opened the door wider and Simba strolled into the room, his tail a question mark. The cat crossed to the bed and jumped up next to Ty, then stood kneading the covers and purring as the boy petted him.

"I think you've made a friend," Josh said.

Ty giggled. "Can he stay, Dad?"

"I don't see why not." Josh tucked the covers around his son, and the big cat stretched out next to the boy, shoving his furry head under Ty's hand.

Ty stroked the cat and yawned again, his eyes beginning to droop. "Promise you'll stay till I'm asleep."

Josh wasn't sure if the request was meant for him or the cat, but he replied, "I promise," and sat back down on the edge of the bed until his son had drifted to sleep.

GEN CURLED UP on the sofa, her legs tucked under her and an afghan pulled over them for warmth. The house had grown chilly since the power went out. She'd stoked the wood stove and the fire was crackling away nicely in it, but it would be a while before the whole house felt its benefits.

She hoped it would be warm enough for Tyler upstairs. Maybe she should offer the McBrides a couple extra blankets. She started to get up, then heard the stairs creak. A moment later, light flooded the stairway as Josh came down carrying the lantern.

"I thought you were going to bed," she murmured, reluctant to speak louder for fear of waking Tyler.

He shook his head. "No, not yet. I guess I'm still too wound up to sleep." He crossed the room and sat down next to her on the sofa. "Ty crashed pretty fast, though."

"I'm not surprised. He had a busy day. You, too," Gen said. "You must have been worried sick about him. I'm really sorry."

"Don't be," he said. "He shouldn't have come here, but it's not your fault he did. Anyway, he's fine, so no use worrying about it." He turned to face her. "Thank you again for opening your home to us. We really appreciate it."

"It's nothing. I'm glad you're here." Gen caught her breath. She hadn't meant to say it aloud, but it was true. "I mean, I'm glad you were able to make it here without getting stranded," she amended. "It's, um, good that you're both safe."

Okay, she thought, how lame did that sound? She needed to shut up now before she said something really stupid.

Josh nodded. "I'm glad we're here, too. Gen, we've gotten off on the wrong foot so many times, and I've jumped to some pretty ridiculous conclusions. Then, well, there was last night. I think we need to talk."

Gen had hoped it wouldn't come to this. That he'd just consider their kiss a mistake and put it behind him. Like she wanted to. No matter how impossible it seemed now. Oh well, she thought, she might as well get it over with. She nodded. "You're probably right."

He fell silent for a moment, and Gen wondered if she should say something first. He was only a couple feet away from her. She could smell the fragrance of his soap, or maybe aftershave, over the tang of iodine disinfectant. He must have performed a late surgery this afternoon.

The mingled aromas reminded her again of last night's kiss. She'd never before thought of iodine soap as erotic. Now the scent would be forever associated with Josh.

She shivered.

Josh must have noticed. "Are you cold?" he asked.

"A little," she replied. "The stove hasn't had much time to heat up the house."

Josh lifted a corner of the afghan and draped it over his legs, then extended an arm toward her. "Here, lean against me."

A part of her wanted to argue, but that rational side of her was easily subdued. She leaned into him and he dropped his arm across her shoulder, gathering her close.

"You did a good job with the hawk." His mouth was close to her ear, his voice low.

"Thanks. I hope he makes it."

"I should have done more." Regret tinged his words. "If I had…"

"If you had, you wouldn't be here now," Gen whispered.

"That's right, I wouldn't." He chuckled, a pleasant sound. "I guess things worked out right after all."

His arm tightened around her and with his free hand, he reached up to lift her chin toward him. His fingers were warm on the sensitive skin of her throat. Then he lowered his mouth to hers.

Chapter Fifteen

Gen surrendered herself to his kiss. Mistake or not, she wanted him to kiss her again. She wouldn't let it go further, she promised herself. It wouldn't be fair to him, to either of them. Even as she thought it, though, she raised her hand to caress the back of his neck, her fingers twining in his hair.

Josh groaned softly, deepening the kiss. His mouth tasted of chocolate, the lingering effect of their cocoa earlier.

A mistake.

Oh, why had she allowed the thought to enter her mind? Now that traitorous part of her, the rational component that had only minutes ago let itself be vanquished, rose to the fore, nagging at her with doubts.

Josh wasn't staying in Halden. He was only here to do a job, then move on. There could be nothing permanent between them. No commitment. Was this really what she wanted?

It wasn't, but it was all she could offer him, especially with her fertility problems. She could love Tyler as her own, but it wouldn't be the same as giving Josh more children.

And what about Tyler, her conscience—or whatever it was—badgered? Was it fair to get attached to him, to let him become fond of her, when he and Josh would be gone in a few weeks' time? How many people had the boy become close to, only to be forced to leave them as soon as his father's job ended?

She pulled away from Josh, gently pressing her hand against his chest. This wouldn't work. It couldn't. Even if she could rationalize it to herself, she couldn't let Ty be hurt because she and Josh were unable to control themselves.

Josh looked at her, his expression questioning, but he didn't speak. He seemed to read his answer in her face and accepted it with a nod.

"I'm sorry," Gen said finally.

He shook his head. "Don't be. It was a bad idea. I'm just glad one of us had the brains to realize it." He rose. "I'll say good-night now. Sleep well."

Gen watched him climb the stairs to his room and knew that this night she wouldn't sleep at all.

JOSH WOKE EARLY the next morning to find Ty sprawled diagonally across the bed, Simba snuggled against him. Josh himself had been relegated to the edge of the mattress, where he lay on his side with one chilled leg dangling over the floor.

He swung himself upright and stretched, groggy after lying awake half the night in a confused state that mingled frustration and anger with a touch of relief.

He didn't blame Gen. She'd been right to push him away. Heaven knows he wouldn't have stopped if she hadn't, despite the fact that he knew it was a bad idea.

Josh stood up and went to the window. The world looked like the inside of a milkshake machine with heavy snow swirled by blasting winds. How long did North Dakota blizzards usually last?

He pulled his cell phone out of his jeans pocket and flipped it on. Still no service, and given the weather, they'd easily be here another night. If not longer. Bad idea or not, he wasn't sure he could stand another twenty-four hours in close proximity to Gen without acting on it.

Unfortunately, hiding in his room all day wasn't really an option. He pulled on his jeans, then walked to bathroom, feeling prickly from a day's growth of beard. He didn't have a razor with him, but that might be an advantage. If he stayed sufficiently scruffy, maybe he and Gen would be able to keep their hands off each other.

He gathered his courage and started downstairs, pulling the door closed behind him so Ty could sleep longer. When he reached the main floor, he heard singing from the kitchen.

Gen's song stopped abruptly as he entered the room, and she glanced at him, her cheeks flushed.

"Don't stop," he said. "You have a nice voice." It was true, and, call him old-fashioned, but there was something very appealing about a beautiful woman singing in the kitchen as she worked.

She did look beautiful this morning, too, in faded jeans and a natural-colored wool sweater, her coppery hair tied back in a ponytail. "Good morning," she said, her smile shy.

Her cheeks were still pink and he realized she wasn't embarrassed about the singing, but about last night.

"Morning," he said. He wanted to say more but, certain he'd only make it worse, he left it at that.

"You're up early."

He shrugged. "Force of habit. Plus Ty had pretty much taken over the bed. I'd have been on the floor in another ten minutes."

"Was Simba in your room? He hasn't come down for breakfast." Gen bustled about the kitchen preparing food for her pets and patients.

Josh nodded. "He's stretched out next to Ty. I think he spent the night with us."

Gen grinned, clearly more comfortable to have a safe topic of discussion. "He likes children. I guess he enjoys the extra attention he gets from them. I hope he wasn't a bother."

"Not at all. Ty wanted him to stay last night and I think it helped him with his fear of the storm." Josh crossed to the back door. "Speaking of which, looks like there's no relief in sight."

Gen stood next to him, but not too close, and he wondered if she was intentionally keeping her distance. "No, it's still going strong," she said. "This is one of the worst I've seen. Unfortunately, it could easily last another day or two."

"Well, at least we're safe." He squinted out at the snow. "I can't even see the Suburban, and I know it's only a few yards from the house. I'd like to get out there and radio the hospital to check in with Beth. She was going to stay the night to keep an eye on an emergency case we got in, and let the Connollys know where I was headed if she was able to reach them."

Gen put a hand on his arm. "It's too dangerous to go out there, even a few yards. The lack of visibility can cause severe disorientation. You might think you're heading back to the house when you're actually moving away from it. People have gotten lost and died of exposure within a few feet of safety."

She glanced at the phone on the wall. "Besides, I doubt if

Beth's been able to reach anyone. My phone and cell are both still out. I've been trying about every hour since I got up."

Josh noted the shadowed areas under her eyes. "How long ago was that?"

"Let's see, it's seven-thirty now. I've been up since about five.

"Force of habit?" he asked.

She nodded. "I'm really not a morning person, if I can avoid it, but when I have animals in the infirmary I like to get an early start. My human patients also have a tendency to wake me in the wee hours for deliveries."

"Yeah, I can see that. Ty was born about two in the morning. Seems like they're always in a hurry to get into the world."

"What happened to Ty's mother, Josh?" Gen asked.

Josh hesitated. Kathy's death was something he hadn't talked about to many people, but if anyone had a right to know, it was Gen. "She died when Tyler was five," he said simply. "Leukemia."

"I'm sorry. That must have been very hard on you both."

He nodded, her look of concern touching him unexpectedly. "It was difficult."

Gen stepped to the counter and took two mugs out of a cabinet. "It's terrible to lose someone you love. I lost my little brother when I was in my teens. He was about Tyler's age. He had a heart defect."

No wonder she had formed such a bond with his son, Josh thought. "Ty must remind you a lot of him."

"Yes, he does. He was a sweet boy, very much like Ty." She poured coffee from a French press coffeepot into the mugs, then handed him one.

"Thanks," he said, realizing she remembered from

meals at the Connollys' that he took his coffee black. The recognition moved him, as did the story of her loss. He felt compelled to offer more.

"I, that is, we've been pretty much on the go since Ty's mother died." He took his coffee and sat down at the table, sliding out a chair for Gen.

She accepted the unspoken invitation and sat beside him. "I got that impression."

"I always thought he was used to it. He seemed to settle in so quickly. Now, I'm beginning to wonder. Pulling him out of school and away from attachments as soon as he makes them—maybe it's not fair to him." Josh didn't know why he was telling her all this, but it seemed like the right thing to do. He cared about her, and he had to let her know why he couldn't allow himself to act on those feelings. He owed her that much.

"I know." Gen didn't prompt him, seeming content to let him fill her in as he saw fit.

"Halden is a great place. It's the kind of town where I could see us making a home." Josh looked up.

Gen was paler than usual this morning, too, he noted. She'd obviously had as bad a night as he. Now he knew he had made the right decision, that her pulling away from him last night had saved them from a serious lapse in judgment.

"But we can't stay here," he went on. "Halden can't support a third veterinarian, even if it was an option. So, I'm thinking that as soon as Sue's ready to return to work, we'll go back to Seattle and maybe I'll start looking for a full-time position." He waited, wondering if she'd protest or give him some kind of indication of her feelings. Hoping she would.

"That makes sense, Josh," Gen said.

She forced a smile, fighting the pain that clenched her in the pit of her stomach.

Get a grip, she told herself. It was no more than she'd expected. She knew Josh would be leaving when his assignment was over. All he'd done was confirm that decision, and give her a good reason for it. He had to consider his son and do what was best for both of them.

She'd made the right choice last night. If it had gone any further it wouldn't have changed anything, only made the inevitable harder on both of them. On all of them.

She took a sip of her coffee, hoping Josh didn't notice the tears that were stinging her eyelids.

The slap of bare feet on the hardwood floor made her look up with surprise.

Tyler came into the kitchen, rumpled and drowsy looking in his jeans and sleep-wrinkled T-shirt. "Morning," he said with a yawn.

"Good morning, Ty," Gen said, grateful for his arrival.

"Morning, buddy." Josh wrapped an arm around his son and pulled him into a hug. "How'd you sleep?"

"Good. Oh!" Ty jumped, then looked down to find Simba twining around his ankles. He gave an exaggerated sigh. "Simba pawed at my head until I woke up. I think he's hungry."

"I'm not surprised. He missed his usual breakfast time." Gen stood up. "Want to help me feed him and the other animals?"

"Yeah!" Ty said, much more awake already.

Gen picked up two full dishes of food from the counter and gestured to the two remaining bowls. "Grab those and follow me. We'll get the whole crowd taken care of."

Simba had already interpreted the direction their conversation was taking. He meowed loudly and circled Gen's legs, then Ty's as the boy picked up the food dishes.

Josh laughed. "I really think that cat has more brains than you give him credit for."

"Like I said, he's pretty bright where food is concerned." Gen led the way, with Simba right behind her, into the infirmary.

With Ty around, she and Josh had no further opportunity to continue their conversation, but Gen found herself relieved. It would have been pointless anyway, she thought. They'd said all there was to say. Nothing could come of whatever attraction they felt for each other. It was best to let it die here.

She plunged into her daily routine, working the McBride men into her schedule. Josh helped her examine the hawk, which was looking much more active and alert this morning. The fox was also improving rapidly, now carrying his weight on the splinted leg.

Gen couldn't exercise the pelican outside today with the blizzard, but let it out of its pen to walk around the treatment area and stretch its legs. Tyler hand-fed it a breakfast of raw minnows. He grimaced at the smell and the slimy feel of the fish, but clearly enjoyed tossing them, one at a time, to the bird, which caught them in its heavy bill.

After the animals were fed and treated, Gen prepared breakfast for the human members of the household. Using her electric griddle for pancakes was not an option with the power off, so she tried her hand at making them on the stove the old-fashioned way.

Busy with cooking and Ty's animated conversation, she could almost forget her talk with Josh and the events of last night.

"Gen, flip them," Ty said as she reached for the spatula to turn the half-cooked cakes.

"I don't know. I've never done that before." She eyed the flat griddle. It didn't look as if it would be that hard.

"Come on," Tyler urged. "They always make it look easy on TV."

Gen glanced at Josh, appealing for help. He shook his head, laughing. "I'm not getting involved. It's your kitchen."

She rose to the challenge. "Okay. Let me loosen them first." She slid the spatula under the cooked side of the pancakes, then lifted the griddle from the burner.

"Just toss 'em in the air," Tyler offered.

"Give me a moment." Gen took a deep breath and flipped the griddle upward with a flick of her wrist.

One of the pancakes rotated perfectly, coming to rest with a small spatter on its uncooked side.

The other pivoted on edge, then dropped off the griddle to land raw-side down on the floor.

Josh and Ty burst into laughter. A moment later, after an appalled glance at the floor, Gen joined them.

"Guess I should have flipped only one at a time." She set the griddle back on the stove and bent to peel the messy half-cooked pancake off the linoleum. "But it's not a very efficient method if you have to cook them one at a time."

"Well, you have a fifty-percent success rate," Josh said. "Want to try for two out of three?"

"Yeah," Ty answered for her.

She shook her head. "No, I think once is enough. I'm obviously not cut out for kitchen acrobatics. Besides, if I keep it up, we won't have enough for breakfast."

At last the pancakes and accompanying bacon were

ready and the three of them sat down to eat, delicious aromas filling the cozy kitchen. Josh could only marvel at how much like a family they seemed, gathered at the table eating and laughing over Gen's pancake-flipping attempts.

He could get used to this, he thought. He couldn't stay in Halden, but maybe Gen could leave with him? He watched her out of the corner of his eye as she joked with Ty, and realized it wouldn't happen. The people of Halden were her family. They needed her. So did their animals. He couldn't ask her to give that up, to give up her home here, for something that neither of them was even sure about.

No, they were better off leaving things as they were. It might hard on them for the remaining weeks of his assignment, but they were adults. They could deal with it.

THE STORM RAGED on throughout the day and into the evening with no sign of letting up. Windblown drifts nearly covered the ground-floor windows on the western side of the house.

"They say snow doesn't melt in North Dakota," Gen remarked as she stirred chili for supper that night. "It just blows around until it wears out."

"I can believe it," Josh said. He opened the back door of the kitchen. Snow had drifted up against the storm door, completely blocking it.

"Wow," said Ty. "We are snowed in. Neat!"

"Well, on this side of the house, anyway." Josh turned to Gen. "How many inches, or would it be feet, have we gotten so far, do you think?"

She looked out the window. "It's hard to say. Probably a couple feet. The drifts make it difficult to tell. You have to find a flat place that's sheltered from the wind to actually measure it. Those are hard to come by out here." She poured the chili into serving bowls. "Okay, dinner's ready. At least with the snow and freezing temperatures, I don't have to worry about the contents of the refrigerator spoiling."

"No," Ty said. "You could just open the glass on your storm door and stick stuff right into the snowdrift."

Gen laughed. "That's a great idea. It makes a lot more sense than carrying snow into the house."

They gathered by lantern light for dinner and another round of Monopoly before it was time for Ty to go to bed.

The wind was just as noisy as it had been last night, but Ty was much less anxious about bedtime. Simba followed him up the stairs and settled on Ty's pillow to wait while the boy brushed his teeth and washed his face. When Ty climbed into bed, placing his new glow stick on the night table, Simba snuggled up against the his side, careful to position himself within easy reach of Ty's hand.

"Dad?" Ty stroked the cat absently, looking up at Josh as he tucked the covers around his son.

"Yep?"

"Can Gen come hug me good night?"

Josh's throat constricted, but he nodded. "I'll go get her."

So much for being adult, he thought as he started down the stairs. He'd been too wrapped up in his own issues to factor Ty's feelings into the mix.

Ty was already attached to Gen. So what could he do about it?

Only one thing made sense. He had to keep Ty from getting any closer to her.

He paused on the stairs, then turned to go back to the bedroom. He'd tell his son she was busy, that she couldn't come up to give him a good-night hug. It might hurt his feelings a little, but in the long run it would be for the best.

Even as he thought it, he realized how wrong it was. He couldn't lie to his son and he couldn't deny Gen the chance to be his friend, especially now that she'd told him about her brother. He was a fool to even think of such a thing.

"Josh?" Gen's voice came to him from the living room.

"Yeah, Gen." He continued down the stairs, stopping at the bottom.

Gen rose from the sofa, her features soft in the dim light of the lantern.

"Ty wants you to come up and give him a good-night hug, if you don't mind." He nodded up the stairs.

Her lips parted in surprise and she smiled, clearly touched by the request. "Oh. Of course." Then she followed him back up to the bedroom.

Chapter Sixteen

Afterward, it occurred to Gen that she should have made up some excuse or done something to avoid seeing Tyler again that night. After all, it wasn't only Josh and she who were involved here. They had Ty's feelings to consider, too, and letting him bond with her would ultimately make leaving more difficult for him. It would make it harder for her, too.

But she couldn't lie or deny herself the joy of being around him.

So she'd hugged him and kissed his cheek, while he wrapped his arms around her neck and squeezed her tight.

"'Night, Gen," he'd said.

She left the room while Josh stayed with him, as promised, until he fell asleep. She went to her own room feeling her eyes burning. She told herself she was just overtired after her late night and early morning and needed a good night's sleep. Too bad the pump wasn't working, she thought, because a hot bath would do wonders, too.

No, that was how she'd gotten into this mess. She closed the door and leaned against it, sighing. With any luck, the storm would blow itself out by tomorrow so Ty and Josh could return to Lilac Hills and their own lives. She could only hope.

A knock at the door nearly made her jump out of her skin. "What?" she asked with more force than she'd intended.

"It's Josh. Can I come in?"

Gen opened the door. Josh stood in the dark hallway. "Come in," she said, and he walked into the bluish glow of the light stick she'd set on her dresser.

"I'm sorry, were you getting ready for bed?"

"No, I was just about to go back downstairs." Gen's breath came rapidly, her insides feeling as if they'd turned to jelly. This was madness, she thought, but she took a step closer to him, unable to help herself.

"Ty's asleep," he said, his voice barely above a whisper. "Thanks for telling him good-night. It meant a lot."

Gen winced but just nodded. It meant a lot to her, too, but he was the last person she'd tell. He stepped nearer and she could smell his masculine fragrance again, that soapy, clean scent that she'd forever associate with him.

She didn't know quite how it happened, but suddenly she was in his arms, her fingers working the buttons of his shirt while his hands smoothed over her back and shoulders, his lips hot against her mouth, her cheeks, her throat.

"Gen, I love you," he murmured, his voice husky with passion. "I don't...I don't know how we can make this work. We shouldn't..."

But even as his words urged caution, he was drawing her closer, his hand finding the hem of her shirt, sliding beneath it to caress the sensitive skin of her back and side.

Her flesh burned at the unaccustomed touch, leaving her trembling. "I know," she gasped against his lips. "But I don't care. I don't care if it ends tonight. I want you."

Gen pushed his unbuttoned shirt from his broad shoulders, baring his hard, muscular chest and arms to her exploration. He released her then, his blue eyes, glowing in the surreal chemical light, locked on hers.

In response to his unspoken question, she nodded, pulling her shirt and bra off together over her head.

She felt wildly wanton as he stared at her, his chest rising and falling quickly as his breathing became rapid. Then he reached for her, pulling her into his arms to claim her mouth with his own, his hands caressing her back, her bottom, her breasts.

Though she could feel the hardness of his arousal straining against the front of his jeans, he seemed reluctant to take her further, as if he was still uncertain that she meant what she said. She reached for his belt buckle, unfastening the belt and the button of his pants, then moving down to the zipper, her hand caressing him unintentionally as she slid it open.

He gasped, then assisted her by pulling off his jeans and briefs in one fluid motion so that he stood before her naked and magnificent.

Josh clasped her against him, lowering his mouth to her throat, then her breasts, to kiss a fiery trail across her flesh as, with his free hand, he stripped off first her jeans then her panties. He surprised her by lifting her into his arms and carrying her to the bed, where he lay her down tenderly.

He stood for a moment, caressing her naked body with his gaze. "Gen, you're so beautiful. I want you so much."

"Josh," was all she could manage. She reached for his hand and pulled him down onto the bed.

GRAY, PRE-DAWN LIGHT filtered into the bedroom, prompting Josh to open his eyes, despite his best efforts to remain asleep. He glanced around the unfamiliar room, wonder-

ing for a moment where he was. Then he remembered.
Gen's room.

And last night…

He rolled over to face the other side of the bed and
found himself alone. He heard sounds of activity from
downstairs. Gen was already up. He stifled his disappointment, forcing himself to think rationally. She had things
to do, and besides, it would be awkward if Ty discovered
them together.

It would be just as awkward if Ty discovered his father
naked in Gen's room. The thought prompted him to swing
out of bed and quickly collect his clothes.

A flicker of motion next to the bed caught his attention
and he realized the clock radio was flashing 12:00. The
power was back on. Now that he made the connection, he
discovered that all sorts of sounds, from the rush of air from
the furnace to the electric hum of appliances, broke the relative silence he'd become accustomed to since the power
failure.

Josh grinned to himself. It had been good with Gen.
More than good. Amazing. But he hadn't expected their
lovemaking to knock the power back on. He found himself wanting to laugh out loud.

He loved her, he realized.

He was in love with Gen. The bald admission was startling in its clarity. Despite all they'd said to each other last
night, there must be some way they could make it work.
There had to be. He couldn't just leave. Not now.

He walked to the window. The storm had subsided and
a blanket of white covered everything as far as he could
see. Mounds had formed, some several feet tall, where
drifts occurred or where objects were buried under the

snowfall. The sky was still gray and threatening, but it appeared the blizzard was over.

Josh dressed and headed downstairs, pausing at the guest room to look in on Ty. His son was still asleep, curled up in a fetal position with Simba tucked between his knees and chest. The yellow cat opened one eye to regard Josh sleepily, as if winking at him, then stretched and lay back down to rest his chin on Ty's arm.

Gen wasn't singing this morning, although Josh had to admit he felt like doing so himself. She was busy at the counter and didn't seem to notice as he entered the kitchen, so he crept up quietly.

When he wrapped his arms around her from behind and leaned down to place a kiss on the back of her neck, she jumped, then he felt her tense in his arms.

"Good morning," he said in her ear, brushing off her stiffness as a figment of his imagination.

"Morning," she murmured, and stepped out of his embrace, turning to him.

She smiled, but he sensed a restraint about her, as if she was purposely keeping her distance.

"Is everything all right?" he asked.

They both recognized the deeper meaning of his question.

Gen nodded. "Fine." She shrugged. "I just woke up too early again."

"It's too early, now." Josh said. "I see we have power, though."

"Yeah, I think it came on about three o'clock."

"You were awake then?" He frowned. He'd collapsed, spent, after their lovemaking. The fact that she'd lain awake alone made him feel like some kind of insensitive clod.

She appeared to recognize his uneasiness and smiled

again, more genuinely this time, he thought. It was a sad smile.

"Don't worry about it," she said.

He couldn't contain himself. "Last night meant a lot to me, Gen," he plunged in, anxious to banish the elephant they were both stepping so carefully around. "It meant a lot to you, too, unless I was sorely mistaken."

Her expression softened. "Last night was incredible, Josh." She looked away. "But it was just, well, last night. We both knew that. This is today and nothing has really changed. You'll be leaving soon and I, I'll be here doing what I've always done. Taking care of my patients, my animals. Being here for Halden."

"I see," he said, a knot forming in the pit of his stomach. The problem was that he did see and he had to admit it. Obviously, her words last night weren't so much an admission that they couldn't have a life together, but that she didn't want one. He was foolish to have thought otherwise. "I guess you're right."

Annoyance welled up in Josh, directed mostly at himself. He didn't know what he'd expected, but she *was* right, and he was the one who was out of line. They'd acted last night knowing there was no future for them, whatever he'd hoped this morning.

It had been so incredible, though. In the light of day, he'd thought that maybe they'd been wrong, that maybe things would work out. Gen clearly had no such illusions.

A part of him wanted to argue, but after all, she hadn't told him she loved him. If she had, things might be different. They might be able to find a way around their dilemma. He knew beyond a doubt that if she loved him, she'd fight for that.

Behind the sadness in her green eyes lay steely resolve. There was no way they could have a life together. She'd accepted that to be the case. It was time he did, too, despite whatever rosy notions he'd awakened with. He had to leave Halden. As soon as possible.

The pain in Josh's expression left Gen feeling as if she'd been punched in the stomach. He really did love her, she realized, just as she loved him.

She wanted to run into his arms, to tell him she was wrong, that there was some way for them to be together, but she knew she couldn't. If she did, she'd regret it. He knew she wouldn't leave Halden, so he'd feel obligated to stay, to try to make some kind of life here for himself and Tyler. She'd be forced to tell him about her infertility, and while he'd probably protest that it didn't matter and he loved her, regardless, ultimately he'd grow to resent her for it. At best, it would only postpone their eventual separation and that would be that much harder on Tyler.

She clenched her teeth and let the pain wash over her, resisting tears but feeling her heart was being torn in half. Then it was done, leaving only a dull, empty ache as Josh gave a curt nod of resignation and turned away.

Gen jumped into the day's routine, feeding and treating her animals, fixing breakfast for Ty, Josh and herself, and washing dishes and clothes, now that both power and water had been restored.

Avoiding Josh was out of the question. They were still trapped in the house. He assisted her with treatments without her asking him and managed to be civil as he did so, while she fought the urge to throw herself at him and beg his forgiveness.

She was a fool.

No, she corrected, she'd been a fool last night. Now she'd come to her senses and set things right. It was hard, but she was doing this for Josh and for Ty. They might not thank her for it, especially Josh, but in the end, she was certain it was the right thing to do.

Shortly after lunchtime, the phone rang. The three of them, sitting in the kitchen, jumped at the unexpected sound. Josh's cell phone jangled at the same time.

Gen launched herself at the wall phone, while Josh answered his cell.

"Gen, it's Sue." Sue Connolly's voice on the other end of the line had never sounded so good. "Are you all right?"

"Sue!" Gen laughed with relief. "I'm fine. Josh and Ty are with me and they're okay, too," she said, anticipating her friend's next question. "How are you?"

"Good. We're all good. I'm so relieved to hear your voice."

Gen could hear tears behind Sue's words. "It's all right, Sue," she said. "We made it through with no problems."

"I know." Sue's voice crumpled and she sniffled loudly into the phone. "Damn hormones. We were frantic about Josh and Ty, especially when we found he wasn't at his friend's house."

"I don't doubt it. We tried to call, but the lines went out so soon after the storm began. How is Matt?"

"Good. He's on the cell with Josh."

Gen glanced at Josh, who grinned, holding up his phone. "Hi, Matt," she called.

"He says 'hi.'" Josh told her.

"Any word on the road conditions?" Gen felt guilty cutting to the chase, but the sooner she had Josh out of her house, the better for both of them.

"The main highways aren't too bad," Sue told her. "The wind blew most of the snow clear of them. It's the side roads that are the problem."

Gen nodded. "As usual. How long before we can get to you, or vice versa?"

Josh glanced up. "Matt says it's supposed to warm up this afternoon. The roads might be passable by tomorrow. What's that, Matt?" He turned his attention back to the phone, then looked at Gen. "He wants to know if you need any provisions? If there's anything you can't do without till tomorrow, he can make a snowmobile run over here tonight."

Ty's face brightened at the mention of a snowmobile. "Really? That would be awesome. I've never seen one up close."

Gen shook her head. "Don't let him come over by snowmobile, Sue," she said into her phone. "His back's in bad enough shape. There's nothing I can't do without till tomorrow or the next day, especially now that the power's back on."

"Aw." Ty was crestfallen. "I really wanted to see the snowmobile."

"Matt says his back is great," Josh relayed on Matt's behalf. "He says he's ready to return to work as soon as the weather clears. Ty, he said to tell you he'll take you out on the snowmobile once we get back to the ranch. This snow's not going anywhere in the next few days." Josh spoke into the cell, "Thanks, Matt. Okay, we'll talk to you tomorrow." He clicked to end the call.

Gen said her goodbyes to Sue and hung up, as well, then breathed a huge, relieved sigh. The Connollys were okay. Now if she could just get the McBrides out of her home and out of her heart.

Josh had several other calls to make now that phone and cell service had been restored. He'd made his decision. He was going to leave Halden. But he couldn't and wouldn't leave the Connollys or their patients hanging while Sue was unable to work. His first call, which he made in the privacy of the guest room, was to an old friend from vet school who owed him a favor.

He left a message with his offer. As soon as he had things arranged, he'd let the Connollys, and Gen, know that he'd be leaving.

His second call was to Beth at the Halden Vet Hospital. The tech had ridden out the storm there, sleeping on the battered sofa in the employee lounge and subsisting on emergency provisions which, strangely, turned out to consist primarily of various forms of chocolate.

Josh attributed that to the fact that four out of five of the hospital's regular staff were women, but he was careful not to say so. In any case, Beth seemed none the worse for her ordeal, and all the patients were fine. Buster was up and walking, eating well and appeared to be on his way to a full recovery.

The rest of the day was filled with errands that had been put off because of the loss of power, along with catching up on weather and news reports. Josh had expected that once they were in contact with the outside world again, he'd feel he'd missed a lot, but in reality, a part of him wished he could stay insulated and content, a part of Gen's household.

He shook off the thought, knowing it was useless to dwell on it. It was best to move on.

Outside, the clouds were beginning to break, allowing pale sunshine to filter through.

"Can we go out in the snow, Dad?" Ty asked.

His son hadn't had a lot of experience with snow, especially this much snow. It was a relative rarity in Seattle and when it did fall, it was usually just a slight dusting.

Josh nodded. "Sure. Bundle up, though. It's about ten degrees out there. I'll get my coat."

"Yeah!" Ty shouted and ran to Gen. "Gen, come outside and play in the snow with us."

She glanced at Josh. "Oh, I don't know. I have a lot to do."

"Pleeeease?" Ty begged. "It won't be as much fun if you don't come out."

Gen relented. "Okay. Let me grab my boots."

They went outside together and Ty immediately began making snowballs, whacking Gen with one solidly in the middle of her back the minute she looked away. She laughed and gathered up a handful of snow to retaliate, plunging through the deep snow to chase him across the yard as he giggled and teased her.

Amidst the ensuing barrage, Josh began excavating the Suburban and Gen's car, but spent most of his time ducking for cover behind them. Before long it was clear that Ty and Gen had decided to form an alliance in the battle for snowball superiority. Ultimately, Josh had no choice but to defend himself.

The vehicles became forts, sheltering each combatant from the other's assaults. Covert ops entered the picture as Ty, taking advantage of his smaller size and greater maneuverability, began sneaking around the end of Josh's fort to make surprise attacks.

By then the outcome was inevitable. With their greater numbers, the foe was able to flank him and Josh found himself caught in a fierce cross fire.

"Do you surrender?" Ty yelled.

"Never!" Josh shouted. "Do your worst, you fiend!"

Laughing, Ty and Gen advanced, pummeling Josh with snowballs until he lost his balance and fell into a massive drift along the side of Gen's car. Ty jumped in on top of him, reaching up to pull Gen down into the drift. The three of them lay there in a pile, laughing and frost-nipped.

The deep-throated roar of an engine shattered the silence. Josh sat up. "What's that?"

"Snowmobile," Gen said. She clambered out of the drift and turned back to offer hands to Josh and Ty, pulling them to their feet, then moved around the front of the car. Josh and Ty followed. "Probably just somone out for a ride. Snowmobiles are pretty popular here, as you might guess."

They watched as the low-slung, red-and-black vehicle approached, more or less taking the path of the snow-covered road to Gen's driveway. The rider wore black from head to toe, an insulated snowmobile suit, Josh could tell as the machine got closer. A streamlined black-and-red helmet covered his head.

The snowmobile was coming to Gen's, there could be no doubt. She glanced at Josh and shrugged, then stepped forward to meet the rider as he pulled to a stop in front of them and dismounted.

The rider unsnapped his chin strap and pulled the helmet from his head. It was Matt.

"Matt," Gen said. "What are you doing here? I told you we were fine on supplies."

Matt's brow was knit with worry. "I'm here for you, Gen. Sue's gone into labor, and it's the real thing this time."

Chapter Seventeen

"How far apart are the contractions?" Gen asked.

"About five minutes." Matt was sweating despite the bitter cold.

"Five minutes?" Gen stared at him in disbelief. "Then she's probably been in labor for hours. She might already be in the active stage. Why didn't you tell me when you called earlier?"

"When they first started, she didn't tell me," Matt said. "She wasn't sure it was actual labor, so she didn't want to worry me about the possibility of having to deliver without you while the storm was going on." He gave an exasperated shake of his head. "As if I haven't helped deliver a few thousand animals. A baby's no different."

He continued, "When the contractions started getting closer together and she realized it was first-stage labor, she wouldn't let me say anything for fear you'd risk trying to reach her while the roads were still dangerous." Matt rubbed his forehead. "She said she wasn't going to have it till you were there, so I decided I'd better come get you."

"What was she planning to do? Keep her knees together?" She sighed. As much as Gen appreciated Sue's thoughtfulness, her friend should have realized this wasn't the time for it. "Did you check for dilation?"

Matt nodded. "She was almost at four centimeters."

"Okay." Gen took a deep breath and let it out slowly. "We've probably got two or three hours till delivery, longer if there are any protractions or arrests in labor, but we'd better get over there quickly. Come in the house. It'll take me just a couple minutes to get my stuff. I'm glad we thought to lay in a tank of oxygen and IV supplies at your place in advance. Somehow I don't think I could get them there on the back of a snowmobile."

She turned to Josh, intending to ask if he'd mind feeding and treating her menagerie while she was gone, but before she could say anything, he spoke up.

"Get going. I'll take care of the animals. We'll drive over tomorrow as soon as it looks like the roads are reasonably clear."

She wanted to hug him, but hesitated. After last night, and more to the point, this morning, she didn't know if she could do it without bursting into tears.

Finally she just said, "Thank you." He nodded and she turned to Ty. "Keep Simba out of trouble for me."

"I will," the boy said.

Gen went into the house to gather her delivery supplies, stripping off her parka and gloves as she went and tossing them onto the living-room sofa.

Matt followed. "You have a snowmobile suit, don't you?"

"Yes. It's in my car with my emergency weather gear. No helmet, though." She collected a pouch of medications from the refrigerator and added them to her bag.

"No problem," Matt said. "I brought a spare."

He glanced at his watch, and Gen could tell he was trying hard to keep his anxiety in check.

"Give me your car keys," he said. "I'll go get your suit."

Gen pulled her keys from her pocket and tossed them to him. "Don't worry, Matt," she said. "Sue's going to be fine."

Josh and Tyler came inside, pausing in the doorway to stamp the snow off their boots and pant legs.

"Is Sue going to have the baby now?" Tyler asked.

"Hopefully not till I get there, but pretty soon." Gen gave him a hug. "Keep an eye on the place while I'm gone."

She turned to Josh. "Help yourself to anything in the fridge or freezer for dinner and breakfast in the morning. The infirmary refrigerator has all the animals' food and there's more in cabinets back there."

Josh nodded. "I've seen where everything is. We shouldn't have any problems."

Matt returned from outside and handed Gen a bulky black nylon bundle. She shook it out to reveal an insulated jumpsuit, which she unzipped and stepped into, pulling it up over her jeans and sweater. She zipped it to her throat, then retrieved her gloves, put them on, and picked up her medical bag, which she stuffed inside a roomy backpack.

"Ready?" Matt asked.

"Let's go," she said. He handed her the spare helmet and she followed him outside, swinging the backpack onto her shoulders.

Gen glanced back at the house to see Josh watching from the door. She pulled on the helmet, securing the strap under her chin, then climbed astride the long snowmobile seat behind Matt. Positioning her feet on the footrests, she wrapped her arms around Matt's waist as he started the engine. Then they were off, kicking up a cloud of powdery snow.

"How are you doing back there?" Matt's shout reached her ears despite the roar of the engine and the insulating effect of her helmet.

She didn't think she could yell loud enough for him to hear her reply, so she stretched her arm over his shoulder and made a thumbs-up sign in front of his face.

They covered the three miles to Lilac Hills much faster than they could have by car with the heavy snow. Matt skidded the snowmobile to a stop close to the house and Gen dismounted. She swung her backpack off her back and pulled off her helmet, then ran up the steps to the front door, Matt close behind her.

She opened the door just as a shriek of pain filled the house.

JOSH DEBATED telling Tyler that they'd be leaving Halden within a couple days. On the one hand, the news would give his son time to get used to the idea. On the other, though, Josh hated the thought of upsetting Ty when he was so happy and so settled.

Wasn't that the problem, though? Half his reason for leaving Halden was to prevent his son from becoming too attached to the place. True, but Ty was a smart kid. He knew they'd be leaving eventually. Best to let him enjoy his stay while he could.

He argued with himself most of the afternoon while Ty watched cartoons and played with the cats, oblivious to his father's internal struggle. At last, Josh decided to wait. Ty would find out soon enough. If he became upset, Josh would point out to him that he'd known they'd be leaving. It was just going to be sooner than they'd expected.

While frozen dinners, scavenged from Gen's freezer,

heated in the oven, Josh prepared the animals' food. He fed them, then treated the fox and hawk while Ty fed minnows to the pelican.

The fox was becoming restless, clearly tired of its confining cage and splint, and Josh narrowly avoided another nip as he examined it. He wished Gen were here to exert her calming influence, then caught himself and forced the thought from his mind.

"I wish Gen was here," Ty said, as if reading his mind. "I miss her. Do you think Sue's had her baby yet?"

"I don't know, son. It can take a while, especially with first-time moms."

Ty tossed the last minnow to the pelican, then turned to lean on the treatment table, propping himself up with his elbow. "Did it take a while for me to be born?"

Josh laughed. "It seemed like forever, but it wasn't too long, actually. You were in kind of a hurry." He gave Ty a little flick on the nose. "And you've been impatient ever since."

"Uh-uh," the boy argued.

"Yeah huh," Josh retorted. He returned the fox to its cage. "Want to go see if dinner's about ready?"

"Yeah, but it won't be the same without Gen." Ty led the way into the kitchen.

"It sure won't" Josh had to agree.

"Okay, Sue, not much longer now." Gen could see that the baby's position was perfect, a cephalic, or headfirst, presentation with the head well flexed, the chin tucked down against the neck. Alignment was good, too. The delivery should go smoothly.

Matt sat behind Sue, holding her in his arms on the bed

in a birthing nest of clean linens layered with plastic, his breathing mirroring her own as she panted between contractions. Hilma bustled about, getting cool, damp cloths for Sue's head, offering her sips of water and doing her best to keep the laboring woman comfortable.

Sue took a swallow of water, then moaned, handing Hilma the cup. "Can I push?" she gasped.

Gen nodded. "Yes, push with the contractions."

Sue's muscles clenched as she bore down, and she cried out against the pain.

"Are you sure you don't want something for the pain, honey?" Matt's face was contorted as he spoke to Sue but looked at Gen for support.

"No. I'm. Fine," Sue managed to grunt the words. The contraction subsided and she forced her breath out in a whoosh. "Remind me again why I'm doing this."

Gen laughed. "You'd be surprised at how often my patients ask that question."

Sue grimaced up at her. "I don't think I'd be surprised at anything at this point."

Gen grinned and smoothed her friend's hair back from her sweaty face, then mopped her forehead with a cool cloth. "You're doing great." She looked at Matt. "Both of you."

At least Matt wasn't on the verge of collapse like Hank Meyers had been, but they weren't done yet. He might surprise her. Sometimes the guys with the most medical experience had the hardest time. It was one thing to encounter pain and bodily fluids in the course of one's job, but something else again to witness them from a loved one.

"Oh, oh, gotta push," Sue gasped as another contraction rolled through her.

Gen checked the progress of the baby. Everything was looking fine and there had been no delays in the labor, but she had fetal monitors, oxygen and other supplies ready in case of any difficulties.

The contraction faded and Sue relaxed.

"You're really close," Gen said. "Not much longer. Do you want to change positions? We can get you upright to squat if you think you'll be more comfortable."

Sue shook her head. "No, lying down is good so far. I thought about that birthing chair thing, but it just seemed too strange."

"A lot of women swear by them. Gravity can be a big help." Gen checked Sue's pulse, then held her stethoscope to Sue's belly to check the baby's heartbeat. They were both within normal limits.

"Unhh," Sue groaned, and shifted restlessly. "I'm sure, but it's still not my style. Maybe with the next one."

"I'll keep that in mind," Gen said. "Or maybe have you try a water delivery."

When the current contraction eased, Sue said, "I'll save that for the third one. By the way, how were your two days stranded with Josh?"

Gen winced. "Have I mentioned that you get mean when you're in labor? Besides, it was two days stranded with Josh and Ty, so it wasn't exactly like a romantic getaway."

"Oh." Sue looked disappointed. "Pretty platonic, huh?"

"Yeah." Gen checked the baby again. The widest part of the head was almost out. "Okay, big push on this next contraction. Matt, why don't you come down to this end? It's nearly show time."

Matt moved out from behind his wife, settling her onto the pillows, while Hilma took his place at Sue's head and grasped her hand. As Matt reached the foot of the bed, a spasm rocked Sue.

"This should be it. Come on, now, push. Push. Push. Push." Her attention never leaving the baby, Gen reached for Matt. She pulled him beside her on the bed, positioning his hands below the baby's head. "Push. Almost there. Push."

Sue bore down, moaning loudly. With a moist, slippery sound, the baby moved out and into Matt's waiting hands.

Gen went into action, suctioning fluid from the baby's nostrils and massaging it to stimulate breathing.

"Congratulations," she said. "You have a beautiful baby girl." She took the baby from Matt and lay her on Sue's chest, careful not to pull the umbilical cord. Matt moved up next to Sue.

"If we can get her to start nursing, that'll speed the delivery of the placenta." Gen helped Sue position the baby. "Don't worry if she doesn't catch on right away, though. Some babies don't and some moms just can't breast-feed. Whatever works out is fine."

Her pain seemingly already no more than a memory, Sue greeted her daughter, cooing and talking to her in hushed tones. She moved the baby to her breast and the tiny infant began to suckle almost immediately. Matt stroked Sue's hair and looked on, his expression one of unbelievable tenderness and amazement.

"Wow, you're a natural." Gen laughed and allowed herself a moment to watch them, knowing she'd never experience that kind of love. Then she shook off the pain of that thought and busied herself with the numerous postpartum details that required her attention.

Chapter Eighteen

The next morning, Josh fed and treated Gen's animals, then he and Tyler climbed into the Suburban for the drive back to Lilac Hills Ranch.

The roads weren't too bad, although a solid freeze overnight had hardened the slushy melting snow to ice. Josh could feel the tires slipping on the frozen surface that underlay the powdery top layer of snow. It was only a couple miles to the ranch, but they weren't going to break any speed records getting there.

Leaving Gen's had been tough on Ty. He'd spent a long time saying goodbye to the animals, especially his buddy, Simba. Josh didn't have the heart to tell his son he wouldn't see the big cat again. He'd let Ty know tonight that they'd be leaving tomorrow.

Josh's veterinary school friend was scheduled to arrive Monday to relieve him at Halden Veterinary Hospital, but if everything worked out well, Josh and Ty would be starting back to Seattle as soon as Ty finished the school day tomorrow, Friday. It was abrupt, he knew, but the weather forecasts were warning of another storm and he didn't want to take the chance of being delayed several days longer. A quick, clean break was best.

They reached the ranch without incident and Josh pulled the SUV into the yard. The front door of the house opened as they were getting out and Matt and Hilma stepped onto the porch.

"You made it," Matt shouted.

"Safe and sound," Josh replied, taking his friend's hand when he reached the porch, then receiving a hug from Hilma. "Congratulations, by the way. Gen called to say it's a girl."

"Thanks. Yeah, she's a doll." Matt put a hand on Ty's shoulder and glanced down at the boy. "Do you want to see her?"

Ty looked thoughtful. "Yeah, I guess so. I wish it was a boy, though."

"Well, maybe the next one will be," Matt laughed, and closed the door behind them.

Sue glanced up from a rocking chair across the living room. "Let me get over this one, first, if you don't mind." She held a tiny bundle swathed in pink blankets. "Come take a look, Ty."

Tyler approached her slowly, as if suddenly shy, and studied the tiny bundle. He turned back to Josh. "Dad, come look at her. She's all red and wrinkly."

Sue laughed. "She is not. She's beautiful."

Tyler made a face and Matt, who'd stepped to his wife's side, smiled. "Between you and me, Tyler, she isn't much to look at yet."

Sue reached out and punched her husband playfully on the arm. "What do you mean not much to look at? She's the image of you, Matt."

"Oh, well then, we're really in trouble. I'd hoped she'd be a beauty like her mom."

Sue beamed. "Okay, you're off the hook this time. But watch it, mister." She looked up at Ty. "Do you want to hold her?"

Ty shook his head, alarm on his face. "No, she's too little. What's her name?"

"Caitlyn Sarah," Sue replied.

Gen came into the room. "Are you sure you don't want to hold her, Tyler? I'll help you."

Ty continued to decline and Gen turned to Josh. "Josh? How about you?"

Josh hadn't expected the offer and he opened then closed his mouth in confusion.

"Sure," Matt agreed. "You've held babies before."

"Well, okay." Josh glanced at Sue. "If you're sure you don't mind."

Sue shook her head. "Not at all. I know babies aren't as fragile as they look, even when they're mine."

Josh had to admit she was right. He knew this tiny, delicate creature had just undergone a process that Kathy had once compared to forcing a bowling ball through a garden hose. It wasn't exactly a gentle experience for either mother or child, and yet in most cases, both endured it remarkably well.

He stepped forward and leaned over Sue, who placed the baby in his arms, then stared down at Caitlyn in amazement as she blew a tiny bubble at him.

Ty looked at her. "She looks like a naked mole rat."

Josh grimaced, but Gen laughed. "No, it's okay. He's right. Most babies do."

"Why's her head pointy?" Ty asked.

"The bones in her skull are soft and aren't joined together, so they can move as she's being born," Josh explained. "Sometimes that makes them stay smushed together for a while."

"Gross. Was my head pointy when I was a baby?"

Josh glanced at Gen to see her biting her lip to keep from laughing. "Yep. It was real pointy."

Ty looked concerned and touched the top of his head. "But it's not now, right?"

Gen and Sue were both laughing now. "No," Gen said, as if unwilling to prolong Ty's worry. "It's not pointy at all now."

Josh settled baby Caitlyn back in her mother's arms. "How are you doing, Sue?"

"I've never been so tired in my life. Or sore," Sue sighed, but she was grinning as she said it. "There are a lot of gruesome little details they don't tell you about in the maternity books, you know." She gazed at her baby. "It was worth it, though. She is beautiful, isn't she?"

"She's gorgeous," Josh replied. "You'll be wonderful parents."

Sue's expression grew serious. "Thank you, Josh. That means a lot."

Josh meant it. He'd grown fond of the Connollys. They were a terrific couple and he regretted having to leave them almost as much as he did leaving Halden. And Gen. He only hoped they wouldn't think badly of him because of it.

He glanced at Gen. She had moved over next to Sue, who handed her the baby. Gen cuddled and cooed over the infant, murmuring softly to her. She'd make a good mother someday, he realized.

The thought hit him like a punch in the stomach. He didn't want to think of Gen as the mother of some other man's child. He couldn't bear the idea of her lying in someone else's arms.

You don't have a lot of choice, a nagging voice in his

mind told him. *She doesn't want you. Just be glad you won't be around to see her with someone else.*

He was glad. By tomorrow evening, he'd be on the road with Tyler, and Gen would be just a memory. She could do whatever she liked once he was gone. He'd never know about it.

For some reason, the thought didn't offer him the relief he expected.

Gen had watched Josh with the baby. As the father of an active eight-year-old boy, he probably knew Caitlyn wasn't as delicate as she looked, but he'd held her as if she were made of porcelain. Gen found herself wondering what it would be like to see him hold a child of theirs. Tears stung her eyelids at the thought.

Stop it, she told herself angrily, *you're only making it worse.* Here she was doing the noble thing, secure in the knowledge it was for the best, and all she wanted to do was ruin everything by throwing herself at his feet and begging him to stay.

"Gen, are you okay?"

Startled, Gen realized Sue was watching her, frowning. She pasted on a smile. "Sure. Why?"

"You looked so sad for a moment."

Gen shook her head in protest. "Just tired, I think. I should probably get home." She turned to Matt. "Can you give me a lift?"

"No problem," Matt replied. "I'll drive you back in the Suburban, since Josh and Ty were able to get through with no trouble." He paused. "Unless you'd rather go by snowmobile?"

"Um, no, thanks." Gen shuddered at the offer. "The truck will be just fine."

"I want to go by snowmobile," Tyler piped up.

"I'll take you out when I get back from Gen's, I promise." Matt turned back to Gen. "Let's get your gear together and we'll hit the road."

Gen collected her supplies, and Matt and Josh helped load them in the SUV, then she said her goodbyes to the Connollys and hugged Tyler. As she climbed into the front passenger seat, she looked around for Josh. He was nowhere to be seen.

Well, she thought, it's for the best. They had already said their farewells. Anything more was unnecessary. She closed the door and Matt started the engine.

WHEN MATT RETURNED from driving Gen home, Josh took the Suburban into Halden to the vet hospital.

"Doc, welcome back!" Beth greeted him from the front desk as he came through the door. "How are the roads?"

"Not bad," he said. "At least between the Connollys' and here. Are you ready to head home?"

Beth stood up. "More than ready. I haven't had a shower for three days."

Josh grinned. "I'll keep a safe distance, then. How are the patients?"

She handed him a stack of charts. "Everyone's doing great. Buster can probably go home as soon as his owner can get here. Greta, too."

Josh groaned. He'd forgotten that the cocker spaniel had been trapped at the hospital after her ear treatment. "Have you heard from Mrs. Gentry?"

"Only about every two hours since the phones came back in service." Beth sighed. "I told her Greta's ready to go as soon as she can get here, but she's worried about driving while the roads are still icy."

"I don't blame her." Josh imagined the elderly woman trying to navigate the treacherous roads. "I hope she'll wait till it's safe. I assume you've assured her that Greta is doing just fine and is perfectly happy to stay till she gets here?"

Beth snorted. "Oh yeah, and Greta actually does seem happy to be here. She can be a nice little dog when no one's messing with her ears. Mrs. G thinks she's pining away, though."

"Well, maybe she'll just appreciate Greta that much more and make an effort to keep her ears cleaned out so this doesn't happen again." Josh flipped through the rest of the folders, then realized Beth was waiting. "You can take off if you like. I'll finish the treatments for today." He paused. "Oh, I don't know what kind of overtime you get for staying seventy-two hours, but I'll talk to Matt and make sure he knows what a great job you did."

"Thanks, Doc." She gathered her coat and purse.

"Drive carefully," Josh said.

"Thanks. You, too." She started out the door.

Josh wondered if he should tell her goodbye. After all, this would be his last day at the hospital. He decided against it since he hadn't even told the Connollys. Somehow this morning had just seemed like the wrong time with the excitement over the new baby, and especially with Gen there.

No, he thought. He'd tell Matt and Sue first, tonight. Then, tomorrow, he'd stop by the hospital on the way out of town and let the rest of the staff know how much he'd enjoyed working with them. He felt like enough of a cad, leaving on such short notice. He couldn't compound that by not even saying goodbye.

JOSH HAD NO OPPORTUNITY to talk to Matt or Sue about leaving once he returned to the ranch. Tyler and Matt were outside and had obviously been busy, judging from the number of snowmen gathered on the front lawn. He found Matt and his son out in the backyard, where Matt was giving Ty an introduction to snowmobiling.

Matt waved Josh over. "You're just in time. I was getting ready to take Tyler for a ride."

"Great," Josh said, hoping he sounded heartier than he felt. Playing in the snow was the last thing he wanted to do in his present mood, but he couldn't disappoint his son. He'd be doing that soon enough as it was.

Tyler pulled on the spare helmet. It was a little oversize for an eight-year-old. Matt grimaced. "Looks like I'm going to have to get a kid-size one."

"Yeah, especially now that you'll have a kid around to wear it." Josh rapped his knuckles against Ty's helmeted head. "Is this safe?"

Matt bent down and tightened the strap under Ty's chin, then tested the fit. "It's good and snug. He's just about big enough for an adult one. We're not going to be doing anything extreme, anyway. Just running around the fields."

"Aw," Ty said. Clearly doing something extreme had been on his agenda. Somehow, Josh wasn't surprised.

Matt mounted the machine, then twisted to face Ty. "Okay, climb aboard."

He turned to Josh. "I'll just run him around the yard, then you and I can trade off so you can give it a try."

"Sounds good." Josh nodded, happy to have an activity to take his mind off his troubles.

Matt started the engine and took off, Ty whooping loudly behind him.

IT WAS NEARLY DARK when Hilma stepped out on the back porch and waved them in for dinner. Ty's cheeks were pink with cold and windburn, and Josh was chilled to the bone. He hustled his laughing son into the house, Matt following after stowing the snowmobile.

Dinner was a quiet affair, with everyone exhausted from the high emotions of the past couple days.

At Ty's bedtime, Josh tucked his son in and kissed him good-night, knowing he had to tell the boy they were leaving and dreading it.

"I miss Simba." Ty rolled onto his side, yawning.

"I know," Josh said. "He's a nice cat."

Ty nodded. "Real nice. I miss Gen, too." He looked up at his father. "Do you?"

Josh wasn't sure how to answer, but found that honesty came naturally. "Yeah. I miss her, too."

"I wish she was my mom," Ty said.

Josh winced. Was he doing the right thing, he wondered for what must be the millionth time? No, you're not, a voice inside said, but you don't have any choice.

"You could marry her, you know," his son went on.

"No, Ty, I can't."

"Why not?"

"Getting married is for people who are in love with each other."

"Aren't you in love with Gen?" Ty asked.

Josh caught his breath. "She's not in love with me." He congratulated himself for deftly sidestepping that one.

"Oh." Ty rolled onto his back and put one arm behind his head, looking suddenly older than his eight years. "Can't you make her be in love with you, like bring her flowers and stuff?"

Josh smiled. Life was a lot simpler in the mind of a child. "It doesn't work that way, son. Either you're in love or you're not. If you're not, flowers and stuff won't help."

"Oh." There was disappointment in Ty's voice. "Even if it's lots of flowers and stuff? Even chocolate?"

"Even chocolate." Josh stood up. This could go on all night, and he knew he'd never have a satisfactory explanation for his son. He bent and kissed Ty's cheek. "It's time for you to get to sleep. You have to get up early tomorrow. It's a big day."

He hesitated at the door, wanting to tell Tyler they were leaving but unable to do so after that conversation. Tonight Tyler was relatively happy. The news that tomorrow would be their last day in Halden could keep a little longer. He left the room, pulling the door closed behind him.

Chapter Nineteen

Josh was tense when he returned to the living room. He'd been dreading this moment. It didn't help that the room was a picture of tranquility, Sue rocking baby Caitlyn, Matt reading the newspaper and Hilma knitting, the click of her needles the only sound in the room.

Taking a seat on the sofa, Josh debated how to bring up the subject, then decided it was best to get right to the point. "Matt, I've decided to leave Halden. Tomorrow will be my last day."

Sue looked up from the baby, confusion on her face. "Tomorrow? Why?"

She'd asked the same questions that were apparently in Matt's mind because he didn't speak, just stared at Josh, puzzled, waiting.

Josh sighed. He wished he could tell them the truth, but there were so many aspects to the truth that it was hard to know what to say. He'd feel like a worse idiot than he did now if he told them it was because Gen had rejected him. In any case, that was only part of the reason.

"I need to find a permanent job and get Ty settled somewhere for good. I like Halden, but I can't make a home for us here. The town can't support another permanent vet.

Thing is, I need to do it as soon as possible, before Ty gets too attached to Halden and, well, to you." He felt sheepish saying it, and worried that it would be painful for them to hear, but it was the truth. At least as much of it as he could tell them. "I always thought he was adaptable, mostly because it was the same kind of life I had as a kid, but I'm finally realizing that this isn't a good life for him."

"I understand, Josh. But it's going to be a while before Sue can return to work," Matt said.

"I know," Josh replied. "I've taken care of that. A buddy of mine from school owes me a favor. Last time I heard from him, he was between jobs, so I called him up and he said he'd be happy to fill out the remainder of my assignment."

He looked from Sue to Matt. "He'll be here on Monday. He's a good vet," he assured them, trying to soften the blow.

Sue just looked stunned. "Monday? But Josh," she hesitated. "Does Gen know?"

Josh flinched at the question. Was it so obvious that there was something between Gen and himself? He had the odd feeling that he and Gen had been the last people to know about it. "She knows I'm leaving. She always knew I would eventually."

Matt stood up. "Josh, we hate to lose you. Really. We've, I mean, Sue and I have enjoyed having you here." He reached for Josh's hand and shook it.

Sue nodded. "We'll miss you. And Tyler."

"I'll miss you, too. I've enjoyed working here, and I'm sorry for the short notice. I can't tell you how badly I feel about it, and I wish there was some other way."

After that, there wasn't much left to say. They made awkward small talk until bedtime, then Josh went to his room.

The door was slightly ajar.

That's funny, he thought. He was sure he'd pulled it closed after tucking in Tyler. With so much on his mind, though, he knew he could have been mistaken. He prepared for bed, but lay awake for a long time before falling into a fitful slumber.

THE NEXT MORNING, he got Ty ready for school as if it were a normal school day. His son was cranky for some reason, though, talking very little and picking at his pancakes at breakfast.

"Looks like someone got up on the wrong side of the bed," Hilma remarked, obviously also noticing the change.

Josh had too much on his mind today to worry about an eight-year-old's bad mood. "Eat up, son, or you'll miss your bus."

Ty gave him a sullen look. "I'm done."

"Okay, then, get your boots on and grab your back-pack." Josh rose and found the backpack himself, then checked his son over to make sure he was well bundled up.

The sun was out, but the snow was still deep on the ground and the temperature below freezing. He kissed Ty's cheek. "Have a good day at school. I'll see you this afternoon."

He noticed that Ty didn't give his usual response as he tromped to the door in his snow boots, but Josh attributed it to his bad mood. The kid was definitely starting to act like a teenager.

Once Ty was gone, Josh sank back into his chair at the kitchen table and nursed his coffee. Packing wouldn't take long. They never traveled with that much to begin with. When he stopped in town to tell the hospital staff goodbye, he'd pick up his lab coat and the few supplies he hadn't brought home the day before.

He wondered if he should stop by Gen's and tell her goodbye? She knew he'd be leaving, but not this soon. Would she be hurt if he left without seeing her again?

She shouldn't be, he thought. After all, it had been her decision to stop things before they went any further.

Then he realized he was being petty. She deserved to know he was leaving, and to be able to tell Ty goodbye.

He was still pondering the best way to tell her when Matt and Sue came into the kitchen together.

They both looked exhausted. He knew the toll a new baby could take on parents' sleep. "Good morning," he said, still uncomfortable and guilty about his news last night.

Sue sat down at the table and Matt stood behind her. "Good morning, Josh." She grinned, dispelling the shadows of sleepiness.

"Morning," Matt said. He was smiling, too.

Wary, Josh raised an eyebrow. What was going on here?

He glanced at Hilma. She had a noticeable smirk. Whatever was happening, they were all in on it.

"Uh, what's up, docs?" Josh asked.

Matt took a deep breath. "Josh, Sue and I had a long talk last night after you went to bed, and we have a proposition for you."

"Oh?"

Matt nodded. Sue was looking up at him and taking her cue from him, said, "Josh, I've decided to make some lifestyle changes. To put it bluntly, I've decided to be a stay-at-home mom for a while. It's something I've been debating, and now it seems like a solution to all of our problems."

"Oh?" Josh said again. He wasn't quite sure where this was going.

"Yep," Matt said. "She's going to stay home with Caitlyn."

"That's nice." Josh still wasn't following. "I think staying home with a baby is a good idea. How long?"

"Till she's in school." Sue glanced up at Matt and winked.

"In school?" Josh thought a moment. "Like, till she's five?"

"Exactly," Matt said.

"Or maybe longer, depending on how I like it and what else happens." Sue added. "Who knows, we might have more kids by then. Gen has me lined up for chair and water deliveries, after all."

"Which means," Matt said, "I'm going to need another vet at the hospital."

"Full-time," Sue interjected. "Permanent."

"And we want it to be you." Matt was beaming even more broadly now.

"Me?" Josh had to wait a moment for their words to sink in. "You're offering me a permanent job?"

Matt nodded. "Yeah, well, you seem to like it here and we like having you. We work well together, and Ty's settled in, and well, there have to be a few other advantages to staying in town."

Josh's breath caught in his throat. The only other advantage he cared about had disappeared with Gen's rejection.

He could live with that, though. Maybe even win her over, eventually. After their time together, he couldn't believe she didn't feel something for him. And in the meantime, he and Tyler would have a home, and he could raise his son in a place he'd grown to love with people he cared about.

There was no way around it. He had to accept.

"Okay," he said, finding he had to force the words out past the lump in his throat. "It's a deal."

"Wonderful!" Sue jumped up and threw her arms around him, while Matt patted him on the back.

Hilma stood grinning at the counter. "Welcome to the family," she said.

Josh could hardly wait for Ty to get home from school so he could tell him the news.

JOSH SPENT the day making arrangements for their relocation. They couldn't stay with the Connollys forever, but both Matt and Sue assured him that he and Ty were welcome for as long as they wanted. Nevertheless, he collected real estate brochures so he could start looking for a place to buy or rent.

Their stored furniture and other belongings wouldn't take up a lot of space, so a little house would be fine for the two of them. Maybe with a nice yard, Josh thought, so Ty could have a dog or maybe a cat like Simba.

He made a point of getting back to the ranch in time to be there when Ty's bus arrived. Usually his son made it home by three-thirty.

Today, three-thirty came and went with no sign of Ty.

Josh double-checked the time with Hilma and Sue, who both were usually in the house when Tyler got home.

"The bus is probably running late," Hilma said. "There's still a lot of snow on the roads."

Sue agreed. "It's probably nothing to worry about, but if he's not home by four, I'll call the school."

By four, Ty still wasn't home. Sue phoned the school. After she hung up, she turned to Josh, a frown knitting her brow. "The buses were running late, but they checked with the driver. She doesn't remember seeing him get on this afternoon. But he *was* in school today."

A cold pall fell over Josh. Where could his son have gone? A possibility occurred to him. *Gen's.*

But why?

The image of the open bedroom door last night flashed before him. He shook his head. Could Ty have heard him telling Matt and Sue that they were going to leave today? It was the only explanation.

Sue was watching him and must have seen the realization dawn. "What is it? Where do you think he is?"

"I think he's gone to Gen's," Josh said. "He told me last night that he wished she was his mom. I think he might have overheard us talking last night."

"When you told us you were leaving?" Sue shook her head. "Oh, Josh. The poor kid."

He pulled his keys out of his pocket. "I'll run over there. The snow should be clear enough for my car to make it now. Can you call and let her know I'm on my way?"

Sue nodded. "Of course." She picked up the phone as Josh ran out the door.

GEN PICKED UP the ringing phone.

"Gen, it's Sue." Sue's voice held an uncharacteristic urgency.

"Sue. Is everything okay? How's Caitlyn?"

"Fine, we're both fine. Gen, Josh is on his way to your house."

"Josh?" Gen was puzzled. "Why?"

"Is Tyler there?" Sue asked.

"Tyler? No. Why would he be here?" A wave of fear rippled through Gen. "Is he missing?"

She heard Sue's sigh on the other end of the line.

"He didn't come home from school," her friend said. "Josh thinks he might have come to you."

"How long ago? Maybe he's on his way but hasn't gotten here yet."

"No," Sue said. "It's been about an hour since he should have gotten home. I'd think he'd be there by now."

"Oh my God, Sue. Do you have any idea why he'd run away?"

"Yeah, I think I do. Last night Josh was talking about leaving today. He'd arranged for another vet to come finish his assignment. We think Ty might have overheard."

Gen caught her breath. "They were leaving today?"

"Well, that's the thing," Sue said. "They were, but now they're not."

"Because Ty's missing?"

"No, because Josh is staying in Halden."

A wave of light-headedness came over Gen. "What?"

"Matt and I talked last night and we decided I should be a stay-at-home mom for a while, which means we need to bring in another vet for the hospital. We offered the job to Josh and he accepted. So he's not leaving, but Ty doesn't know that."

Gen sank to her knees beside the kitchen counter. Josh wasn't leaving.

He and Ty were staying in Halden.

And he was on his way to her house.

"Gen, are you there?" Sue asked, concern in her voice.

"I'm here." Gen tried to force the confusion of thoughts from her mind. Josh was staying, but Ty was missing. Icy cold clenched at her insides. Where could he have gone? "How long ago did Josh leave your place?"

"About ten minutes, so he should be there any moment. He's in his car, but he's taking it slow."

"Okay." Gen managed to get back on her feet. "We need to start a search. The weather's supposed to get snowy again, and even if it doesn't, it'll be bitter cold out there as soon as it gets dark."

"You're right. Oh heavens, I hadn't even considered that he wouldn't be with you." Sue's voice rose, taking on an edge of panic.

"Is Matt home?" Gen asked.

"No, he's at the hospital, but I'll call him. He can check along the way from Halden to your house."

"Good." Gen thought for a moment. "Better call the sheriff, too. If Tyler didn't stick to the main roads, we might need to search by snowmobile." She heard the slam of a car door outside. "Sue, I think Josh just got here. Go ahead and make those calls, then call us back."

She hung up and ran to the front door, opening it before Josh could knock.

He gaped in surprise. "Gen, where's Ty?"

"I just got off the phone with Sue," she said. "Josh, he's not here."

"What?" Josh stared in disbelief. "I was sure he'd come here. After what he said last night."

She shook her head. "I haven't seen him, and I'm sure he'd have gotten here by now if this was where he planned to go."

"You're right." His face crumpled. "Where could he have gone?"

"I don't know." She took Josh's arm and led him into the house. "Sue's calling Matt and the sheriff. They'll search between Halden and here, in case he's just following the road."

"I was such an idiot," Josh said. He sank down on her

sofa, his head in his hands. "I had no idea he'd overhear. I thought he'd gone to sleep."

"It's okay. We'll find him." Gen sat beside him and put her hand on his shoulder. "What did he say last night? Maybe it'll give us some idea."

Josh turned to face her, his eyes red rimmed. "He said he wanted you to be his mom." He gave a painful laugh. "He said I should marry you."

Gen's breath caught in her throat. "Oh, Josh."

"I know," he said. "I told him that people were either in love or they weren't and since you weren't, well…" He shrugged. "It just wouldn't work out."

Gen swallowed, a lump the size of an egg in her throat. "What did he say?" she managed.

Josh laughed again. "He said maybe I could give you lots of flowers, or chocolate, to make you love me back."

Tears sprang to Gen's eyes and she bit her lip. "Josh, it wouldn't require any of those things for me to love you back."

"Yeah, I told him it didn't work that way." He paused, then looked at her. "What?"

Gen shook her head. "I said I don't need flowers or candy to make me fall in love with you. I'm already in love with you."

"What?"

"Only two whats? You're not very bright." She laughed. "I'll spell it out for you." She took his face in her hands. Nothing else mattered. She loved him and she'd tell him so. She'd tell him everything and let the chips fall where they may. "Josh, I am in love with you. I don't need anything else to make me feel this way."

"But, I thought, I mean, what about 'last night was just last night and nothing has changed'?"

"You were leaving, Josh." Gen stood up. "And I…" She dropped her gaze. "I was afraid to tell you how I felt. I was afraid you'd give up your career and try to make a life here, and I knew that wouldn't be fair to you." She looked up again, feeling the tears slide down her cheeks. "You see, Josh, I was sick a few years ago, and the doctors tell me I'll never be able to get pregnant. I couldn't tell you I loved you and then have you change your whole life, only to find out, afterward, that I could never bear your children."

"But you are in love with me?" Understanding was dawning at last.

She nodded, wiping the moisture from her cheeks. "I'm in love with you."

He rose and pulled her into his arms. "Gen, darling, I already have a child, and he wants you to be his mother. *I* want you to be his mother. If we can't have other children together, it doesn't matter. We'll be a family. We love you."

Gen felt a flutter of hope rise in her chest. "Are you sure, Josh? You don't have to do this."

In answer, Josh tightened his embrace and lowered his mouth to hers, kissing her deeply. "I'm sure. I think I've been sure since the first time I met you. I just didn't want to admit it to myself. I've been an idiot. It's been so long since I've let anyone but Tyler into my life."

He shook his head. "I was an idiot about him, too. I had no idea what I was doing to him, moving him around all the time, making him pay for the stuff I couldn't put behind me. No wonder he ran away." He looked into Gen's eyes. "But I have put it behind me. Gen, how can I ever make it up to him?"

"You will," Gen said. "You already have. But now we have to find him."

He caught his breath and nodded. "You said Matt and the sheriff are searching from Halden? What if they don't find him?"

"Sue told me they might need to initiate a search by snowmobile if there's any chance he might have gone cross-country."

Josh shuddered. "Oh, God, I was so sure he was here. Now, he might be out in the snow somewhere." He took her hand. "Come on, we'll take my car and start looking from this direction. He might still be on his way here."

Gen reached for her coat. "I'll leave the door unlocked and a note to call my cell if he gets here." She found a piece of paper and wrote out the note, then taped it to the door.

TWO HOURS LATER, it was fully dark and the temperature had fallen into the teens. There was still no sign of Ty and searchers were out on snowmobiles looking for him.

Gen and Josh had returned to her house after their fruitless search, hoping that Ty might at last be there, but with no luck. After waiting another hour, they decided their best course was to return to Lilac Hills and wait for news from the professionals.

HILMA HAD FIXED DINNER, but hardly anyone had had an appetite. All they could think about was an eight-year-old boy, lost, cold and probably hungry, somewhere out in the snow.

"I can't just sit here," Josh said, pacing the kitchen. He turned to Matt. "Maybe we should take the truck out again, or I could take the snowmobile?"

Gen put a hand on his arm. "They're patrolling the roads, so if he's there, someone will find him. And you don't know the terrain, so taking a snowmobile out might end up with you getting lost, too."

Matt nodded. "She's right. We don't want to be searching for both of you."

"Well, I have to do something." Josh shrugged. "Anything to keep my mind off the time passing."

Hilma spoke up. "Tessie hasn't had her feeding yet tonight. We were all too busy with the search and forgot about her. If you want to, you can go on out to the barn and give her a flake of hay and some grain."

Gen nodded. "It won't kill a lot of time, but at least it's something to do."

"Okay," Josh agreed. He reached for Gen's hand, unwilling to let her, too, out of his sight.

He tried not to think about Ty, knowing, logically, that worry wouldn't solve anything. Still, he tried to remember if he'd made his son bundle up sufficiently, if Ty had been wearing his snow boots. Did he have his gloves with him?

Was he hungry? Josh hoped to God Ty was hungry, because if he wasn't…

He shook off the thought, unwilling to face it. "Come on," he told Gen.

They pulled their coats on and walked out to the barn together.

Sheltered from the wind and well insulated with a good supply of hay, the barn was surprisingly warm. Josh went to the feed area where several bales were kept for daily feeding. He pulled off a flake from an open bale.

Gen scooped up a bucket of grain and glanced at the water faucet and scrub sink. "I wonder how she's doing for water?" she said.

"We can come back for it if she needs it," Josh said.

Together they carried the food to Tessie's stall. The white bison calf heard their approach and pressed against the front rail, snorting, anxious for her food. She rested her head on top of the upper rail to greet them, asking for a head scratch.

"Beggar," Gen said, laughing. She climbed up on the rail and poured the grain into Tessie's feed trough as Josh hefted the hay flake into its rack. Dust and bits of hay cascaded down from the rack into the bottom of the stall.

Something rustled in the straw behind the bison. Then it sneezed. Gen gasped in surprise and leaned over the railing as a small figure shook itself free of the straw.

"Tyler," Josh shouted. He vaulted over the rail, startling Tessie who shied to one side.

Gen caught the bison calf's head and held her, making soothing noises. Tessie calmed under her touch.

Josh gathered his son in his arms. "Ty, where have you been? Everyone's out searching. We've been worried sick."

"I've been right here. I guess I fell asleep," the boy said matter-of-factly. "I didn't want to go. Dad, do we have to go? I want to stay here."

Josh looked down at his son, then over at Gen. He held out his hand to her. Gen climbed over the railing and joined the McBride men in the straw. Josh took her hand. "No, Ty. We don't have to go anywhere. We're already home."

Epilogue

One year later

Spring came early to Halden and, as usual this time of
year, Halden Veterinary Hospital was swamped with
appointments.

An exhausted Josh McBride pulled his Volvo in behind
Matt's Suburban, eager to see Gen and Tyler, who had
spent the day at the ranch while Ty had the day off from
school.

Sue stepped onto the front porch, one-year-old Caitlyn,
a curly-haired bundle of energy, squirming in her arms.
"They're out at the barn, Josh," she said. "A new bison calf
was born this morning."

She came down the steps to greet him. "I was just heading out there. Cait loves the barn. I don't know how I'm
going to keep her out of it once she's walking on her own."

Josh laughed. "Just start giving her chores out there.
That'll make her keep her distance. So, Tessie has a sister
or brother?"

"Brother," Sue said. "He's not white, but we didn't expect that. Tessie's a rarity. He's adorable, though."

They walked together to the barn. Matt was in the stall

with the bison cow and her calf, checking both animals to make sure they were healthy. Gen and Tyler stood at the rail watching.

Tyler looked up at his approach. "Dad, come see. Tessie's mom had her baby, and I got to see it born."

Gen turned to Josh and smiled. "It's lucky he had the day off. He came out here the first thing when we arrived, just in time for the delivery."

Josh joined them at the stall. The bison calf was small, pale brown and fuzzy. At this age, it didn't have the massive head and hump that it would develop as it reached adulthood, so it bore little resemblance to its huge mother.

Simply looking at the animals seemed to refresh Josh's tired body. He couldn't help grinning as Matt released the calf and it moved on thin, unsteady legs back to the security of its mother's side.

Gen put a hand on his arm and her touch further restored him. "Hard day, hon?" she asked.

"Insane," Matt said.

"'Tis the season," Josh agreed. "Oh well, a few more weeks and everything will be back to normal."

He looked up to catch an exchange of glances between Gen and Sue. Both of them were grinning.

"What?" he said, wary. His wife and Sue had been friends for a long time, and when the two of them got together, there was no telling what might happen.

Sue laughed. "I can't stand it, Gen. Tell him, or I will."

Gen turned to Josh and put her arms around his neck.

Puzzled, he looked into her green eyes that now sparkled with mischief.

"I didn't want to say anything until I was sure," she said, "but it looks like the laser treatments Dr. Lansing recommended worked." She reached down to pat her flat tummy. "I'm afraid your baby season isn't going to be over for a while yet."

* * * * *

Welcome to the world of American Romance!
Turn the page for excerpts from our April 2005 titles.

SPRING IN THE VALLEY by Charlotte Douglas

DISCOVERING DUNCAN by Mary Anne Wilson

MAD ABOUT MAX by Penny McCusker

LOVE, TEXAS by Ginger Chambers

We're sure you'll enjoy every one of these books!

Spring in the Valley (#1061) is the third book in Charlotte Douglas's popular series A PLACE TO CALL HOME. The previous titles are *Almost Heaven* and *One Good Man*.

When you read *Spring in the Valley,* you'll meet local police officer Brynn Sawyer and New York City attorney Rand Benedict, who's come to Pleasant Valley with his orphaned nephew. Brynn and Rand quickly develop a relationship—but Rand has a secret agenda that's going to affect not only Brynn but the whole town. Still, Rand will find himself enchanted by Pleasant Valley…. It's the kind of place where neighbors become friends and where people care—small-town life as it was meant to be!

Hiking her long silk skirt above her boots, Officer Brynn Sawyer slid from the car and used her Mag-Lite to guide her steps to the idling Jaguar she'd pulled over. At her approach, the driver's window slid down with an electronic whir.

The driver started to speak. "I have a—"

"I'll do the talking. This is a state highway, not a NASCAR track," Brynn said in the authoritative manner she reserved for lawbreakers, especially those displaying such an obvious lack of common sense. "And the road's icing up. You have a death wish?"

"No." The driver seemed distracted, oblivious to the seriousness of his offense. "I need to—"

"Turn off your engine," Brynn ordered, "and place your hands on the wheel where I can see them."

She shined her flashlight in the driver's face. The man, who was in his mid-thirties, squinted in the brightness, but not before the pupils of his eyes, the color of dark melting chocolate, contracted in the light. She instantly noted the rugged angle of his unshaven jaw, the aristocratic nose, baby-fine brown hair tousled as if he'd just climbed out of bed…

And a wad of one-hundred-dollar bills thrust under her nose.

Anger burned through her, but she kept her temper. "If that's a bribe, buster, you're in a heap of trouble."

"No bribe." His tone, although frantic, was rich and full. "Payment for my fine. I can't stop—"

"You can't keep going at your previous speed, either," she said reasonably and struggled to control her fury at the man's arrogance. "You'll kill yourself and someone else—"

"It's Jared. I have to get him to the hospital."

Labored breathing sounded in the back seat. Brynn aimed her light at the source. In a child carrier, a tow-headed toddler, damp hair matted to his head and plump cheeks flushed with fever, wheezed violently as his tiny chest struggled for air.

Brynn's anger vanished at the sight of the poor little guy, and her sympathy kicked in. She made a quick decision.

"Follow me. I'll radio ahead for the E.R. to expect us."

With *Discovering Duncan* (#1062), Mary Anne Wilson launches a brand-new four-book series, RETURN TO SILVER CREEK. In these stories, various characters return to a Nevada town for a variety of reasons—to hide, to come home, to confront their pasts. In *Discovering Duncan,* a young private detective, Lauren Carter, is hired to track down a wealthy client's son. When she does so, she also discovers the person he really is—not to mention the delights of this small mountain town!

"I'm a man of patience," D. R. Bishop said as his secretary left, closing the door securely behind her. "But even I have my limits."

Lauren Carter never took her eyes off the large man across from her at the impressive stone and glass desk. D. R. Bishop was dressed all in black. He was a huge, imposing man, and definitely, despite what he said, a man with little patience. He looked tightly wound and ready to spring.

Lauren sat very still in a terribly uncomfortable chair, her hands in her lap while she let D. R. Bishop do all the talking. She simply nodded from time to time.

"My son walked out on everything six months ago," he said.

"Why?"

He tented his fingers thoughtfully, with his elbows resting on the polished desktop, as if he were considering her single-word question. But she knew he was considering just how much to tell her. His eyes were dark as night, a contrast to his snow-white hair and meticulously trimmed beard. "Ah, that's a good question," he said. For some reason, he was hedging.

"Mr. Bishop, you've dealt with the Sutton Agency enough to know that privacy and discretion are part of our service. Nothing you tell me will go any farther."

He shrugged his massive shoulders and sank back in his chair. "Of course. I expect no less," he said.

"So, why did your son leave?"

"I thought it was a middle-age crisis of some sort." He smiled slightly, a strained expression. "Not that thirty-eight is middle-aged. Then I thought he might be having a breakdown. Maybe gone over the edge." The man stood abruptly, rising to his full, imposing height, and she could've sworn she felt the air ripple around her from his movement. "But he's not crazy, Ms. Carter, he's just damn stubborn. Too damn stubborn."

She waited as he walked to the windows behind him and faced the city twenty floors below. When he didn't speak, she finally said, "You don't know why he left?"

The shoulders shrugged again. "A difference of opinion on how to do business. Nothing new for us." He spoke without turning. "We've always clashed, but in the end, we've always managed to make our business relationship work."

"What exactly do you want from the Sutton Agency, Mr. Bishop?"

"Find him."

"That's it?"

He turned back to her, studying her intently for several moments before he said, "No."

"Then what else do you want us to do?"

"As an employee of Sutton, I want you to find my son. I also want him to come back willingly."

"Okay," she said. She'd handle it. She had to. Her future depended on finding the mysterious Duncan Bishop.

We're thrilled to introduce a brand-new writer to American Romance! *Mad About Max* (#1063) is the first of three books by Penny McCusker. They're set in Erskine, Montana, where the residents gather at the Ersk Inn to trade gossip and place bets in the watering hole's infamous betting pools. Cute, klutzy schoolteacher Sara Lewis is the current subject of one of the inn's most popular pools ever. She's been secretly (or not so secretly!) pining for rancher and single dad Max Devlin for going on six years, and this story sees her about to take her destiny into her own hands. Penny writes with the perfect mix of warmth and humor, and her characters will have you cheering for them right to the end.

"Please tell me that wasn't Super Glue."

Sara Lewis tore her gaze away from the gorgeous—and worried—blue eyes of Max Devlin, looking up to where her hands were flattened against the wall over his head. Even when she saw the damning evidence squished between her right palm and her third-grade class's mangled Open House banner, she refused to admit it, even to herself.

If she admitted she was holding a drained tube of Super Glue in her hand, she might begin to wonder if there'd been any stray drops. And where they might have landed. That sort of speculation would only lead her to conclusions she'd be better off not drawing, conclusions like there was no way a stray drop could have landed on the floor. Not with her body plastered to Max's. No, that kind of speculation would lead her right into trouble.

As if she could have gotten into any more trouble.

She'd been standing on a chair, putting up the banner her third-grade class had created to welcome their parents to Erskine Elementary's Open House. But her hands had jerked when she heard Max's voice out in the hallway, and she'd torn it clear in half. She'd grabbed the first thing off her desk that might save the irreplaceable strip of laboriously scrawled greetings and brilliant artwork and jumped back on her chair, only to find that Max had gotten there first. He'd grabbed one end of the banner, then dived for the other as it fluttered away, ending up spread-eagled against the wall, one end of the banner in either hand, trapped there by Sara and her chair.

She'd pulled the ragged ends of the banner together, but just as she'd started to glue them, Max had turned around and nearly knocked her over. "Hold still," she'd said sharply, not quite allowing herself to notice that he was facing her now, that perfect male body against hers, that heart-stopping face only inches away. Instead, she'd asked him to hold the banner in place while she applied the glue. The rest was history. Or in her case infamy.

"Uh, Sara…" Max was trying to slide out from between her and the wall, but she met his eyes again and shook her head.

"Uh, just hold on a little longer, Max. I want to make sure the glue is dry."

What she really needed was a moment to figure out

how badly she'd humiliated herself this time. Experimentally, she stuck out her backside. Sure enough, the front of her red pleather skirt tented dead center, stuck fast to the lowermost pearl button on Max's shirt—the button that was right above his belt buckle, which was right above his—

Sara slammed her hips back against his belly, an automatic reaction intended to halt the dangerous direction of her thoughts and hide the proof of her latest misadventure. It was like throwing fuel on the fire her imagination had started.

Blood rushed into her face, then drained away to throb deep and low, just about where his belt buckle was digging into her—

"Sara!"

She snapped back to reality, noting the exasperation in his voice, reluctantly she arched away from him. The man had to breathe, after all.

"There's a perfectly reasonable explanation for this," she said in a perfectly reasonable voice. In fact, that voice amazed her, considering that she was glued to a man she'd been secretly in love with for the better part of six years.

"There always is, Sara," Max said, exasperation giving way to amusement. "There was a perfectly reasonable explanation for how Mrs. Tilford's cat wound up on top of the church bell tower."

Sara grimaced.

"There was a perfectly reasonable explanation for why Jenny Hastings went into the Crimp 'N Cut a blonde and came out a redhead. Barn-red."

Sara cringed.

"And there was a perfectly reasonable explanation for the new stained-glass window in the town hall looking more like an advertisement for a brothel than a reenactment of Erskine's founding father rescuing the Indian maidens."

She huffed out a breath, indignant. "I only broke the one pane."

"Yeah, the pane between the grateful, kneeling maidens and the very happy Jim 'Mountain Man' Erskine."

"The talk would die down if the mayor let me get the pane fixed instead of just shoving the rest of them together so it looked like the Indian maidens were, well, really grateful."

"People are coming from miles around to see it." Max reminded her. "He'd lose the vote of every businessman in town if he ruined the best moneymaker they've ever had."

Sara just huffed out another breath. It was a little hypocritical for the people of Erskine, Montana, to pick on her for something they were capitalizing on, especially when she had a perfectly good reason for why it had happened, why bad luck seemed to follow her around like a black cloud. Except she couldn't tell anyone what that reason was, especially not Max. Because he was the reason.

Veteran author Ginger Chambers returns to American Romance with *Love, Texas,* a warm, engrossing story about returning to your past—coming home—and seeing it in an entirely new way.... You'll enjoy Ginger's determined and delightful heroine, Cassie Edwards, and her rancher hero, Will Taylor. Cassie is more and more drawn into life at the Taylor ranch—and you will be, too. Guaranteed you'll feel right at home in Love, Texas!

When Cassie Edwards arrived at the Four Corners—where Main Street was intersected by Pecan—nothing in Love, Texas, seemed to have changed. At Swanson's Garage the same old-style gasoline pumps waited for customers under the same rickety canopy. The Salon of Beauty still sported the same eye-popping candy-pink front door. Handy Grocery & Hardware's windows were plastered with what could be the same garish sale banners. And from the number of pickup trucks and cars crowded into the parking lot on the remaining corner, Reva's Café still claimed the prize as the area's most popular eating place.

Old feelings of panic threatened to engulf Cassie, forcing her to pull the car onto the side of the road. She had to remember she wasn't the same Cassie Edwards the people of Love thought they knew so well. She'd changed.

Cassie gripped the steering wheel. She'd come here to do a job—to negotiate a land deal, get the needed signatures, then get out…fast!

A flutter of unease went through her as her thoughts moved to her mother, but she quickly beat it down. She'd known all along that she'd have to see her. But the visit would be brief and it would be the last thing she did before starting back for Houston. She glanced in the rearview mirror and pulled back out onto Main and continued toward the Taylor ranch.

Cassie drove down the highway, following a line of tightly strung barbed wire that enclosed grazing Black Angus cattle. The working fence ran for about a mile before being replaced by a rustic rock fence that decorated either side of a wide metal gate, on which the ranch's name, the Circle Bar-T, was proudly displayed in a circle of black wrought-iron. A sprawling two-story white frame house with a wraparound porch sat a distance down the driveway, the rugged landscape around it softened with flowers and more delicate greenery.

Cassie hopped out of the car, swung open the gate and drove through.

"Hey!" a man shouted.

Cassie looked around and saw a jeans-clad man in a long-sleeved shirt and bone-colored hat heading toward her, and he didn't look pleased. She'd had a thing for Will Taylor when she'd first started to notice boys. Trim and athletic with thick blond hair and eyes the same blue as the Texas sky, he was handsome in the way that made a girl's heart quicken if he so much as looked at her. But even if he had noticed her in the same way she'd noticed him, there'd been a gulf between them far wider than the difference in their ages. She was Bonnie Edwards's daughter. And that was enough.

"You forgot somethin', ma'am," he drawled. "You didn't close the gate. In these parts if you open a gate, you need to close it."

Will Taylor continued to look at her. Was he starting to remember her, too?

He broke into her thoughts. "Just go knock on the front door. My mom's expectin' you." Then, with a little nod, he stuffed his hat back on his head and walked away.

Cassie stared after him. Not exactly an auspicious beginning.

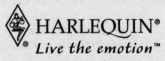

If you enjoyed what you just read,
then we've got an offer you can't resist!

Take 2 bestselling
love stories FREE!

Plus get a FREE surprise gift!

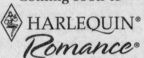
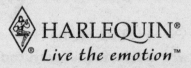